Charlotte,

I know I'll probably never be able to make it up to you and your family—my family—for what I did to you and the Hotel Marchand back in New Orleans, but somehow I'm going to try. That's why it's important to me to keep in touch with you.

I think our grandmother Celeste meant to punish me by sending me out here to Cajun country, but even she's got to be happy with the way things are going. Her old Creole cottage, La Petite Maison, is now a beautiful B and B with paying guests. I never thought of myself as a small-town innkeeper, but I have to admit, the village of Indigo is growing on me. You'd love the little opera house the locals are hoping to restore, and you can't beat the turtle soup and gumbo. There are some real characters in the town, but I have to admit, their friendliness is still something I'm not used to. The only one who looks at me with suspicion is Alain Boudreaux, the chief of police, but since he knows my past, I can hardly blame him. Let me know how you and your sisters are doing, and give my love to Aunt Anne. One day I'll make you proud to have me in the family.

Luc

Carroll, Marisa
            Her summer lover.

Dear Reader,

Marian and I live nearly a thousand miles north of Indigo, Louisiana, but the town itself is very familiar to us. It is filled with hardworking men and women to whom family and country mean a great deal. Neighbors look out for each other and rejoice in the good times and comfort each other during the bad ones.

But even the residents of an idyllic small town like Indigo have to face the realities of life in the twenty-first century—including the high cost of health care and prescription drugs.

That's why chief of police Alain Boudreaux's mother and grandmother decide, with the help of a few friends, to begin smuggling their medications across the border from Canada. It saves everyone a bundle of money and isn't really *too* illegal. The plan works fine until Sophie Clarkson, Alain's first love, arrives back in town to settle her godmother's estate and stumbles onto the scheme.

Then all heck breaks loose.

Won't you please join us in Indigo and...*laissez les bons temps rouler!*

Carol and Marian

HOTEL MARCHAND

MARISA CARROLL

Her Summer Lover

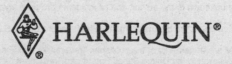

HARLEQUIN®

TORONTO • NEW YORK • LONDON
AMSTERDAM • PARIS • SYDNEY • HAMBURG
STOCKHOLM • ATHENS • TOKYO • MILAN • MADRID
PRAGUE • WARSAW • BUDAPEST • AUCKLAND

ISBN-13: 978-0-373-38946-9
ISBN-10: 0-373-38946-9

HER SUMMER LOVER

Copyright © 2006 by Harlequin Books S.A.

Carol Wagner and Marian Franz are acknowledged as the
author of this work.

This edition published by arrangement with Harlequin Books S.A.

® and TM are trademarks of the publisher. Trademarks indicated with
® are registered in the United States Patent and Trademark Office, the
Canadian Trade Marks Office and in other countries.

www.eHarlequin.com

Printed in U.S.A.

Marisa Carroll is the pen name of authors Carol Wagner and Marian Franz. The team has been writing bestselling books for nearly twenty-five years. During that time they have published over forty titles, most for the Harlequin Superromance line, and are the recipients of several industry awards, including a Lifetime Achievement award from *Romantic Times BOOKclub* and a RITA® Award nomination from Romance Writers of America. The sisters live near each other in rural northwestern Ohio surrounded by children, grandchildren, brothers, sisters, aunts, uncles, cousins and old and dear friends.

PROLOGUE

Indigo, Louisiana, January, 1900

AMELIE VALOIS stood in the cold, misting rain of the late-January afternoon and looked at the beautiful little opera house her Alexandre had built for her so many years before. She lifted the heavy silk veil that had shielded her from the curious eyes peering from behind lace curtains across the square. What did it matter if strangers saw her tears? She cried for him, for herself, for the loneliness of the years she'd spent without him.

Alexandre Valois, her husband, her lover. Dead of a nameless fever in a Yankee prison camp, nearly forty years in his grave. He would be an old man now, as she was an old woman, no longer the dashing young Creole gentleman who had swept her off her feet and married her, against the wishes of his wealthy family, and her own, oh, so long ago.

She lifted her long wool skirts and accepted the hand of the rail-thin black man who stood waiting patiently at the carriage door. "*Merci*, Titus," she said.

"You're welcome, Miss Amelie." As a boy Titus Jefferson had been a slave on her in-laws' indigo plantation. Now he owned a livery stable on property that he had once labored on. Not all the changes time wrought were bad ones, she reminded herself.

She tilted her head to look at the building, designed for her husband by the famous New Orleans architect, James Gallier, Jr. The whimsical copper weathervane still graced the pinnacle of the cupola on the roof; the brickwork was in good repair; the cypress pillars that supported the wrought-iron balcony freshly white-washed. The glass panes of the huge carriage lamp that hung above the carved double doors were polished, gleaming fitfully in the gray afternoon light. "It looks good, Titus."

"Yes, ma'am. The Lesatzes, they take good care of it. Bring in some money for the town, too. Had two revival meetings here last year with a preacher man out of Baton Rouge. So many people came that every spare room for three miles 'round was rented out. And they're talking about a Vaudeville troop coming all the way down from Chicago come spring."

"Vaudeville?" She looked up into his dark, leathery face with a wry smile. "Oh, dear. Well, at least there will be music."

"Just like the old days when you used to sing here, Miss Amelie. I remember all us field hands listening outside when the windows was open. You sure did have a nice voice, Miss Amelie. Like an angel singin'. I sure would like to hear you sing again."

"I'm afraid my singing days are past, Titus. But thank you for remembering."

"Do you want to go inside now?"

She laid her arm on his and stepped heavily from the carriage. Even the short walk to the three shallow steps that spanned the width of the pillared entry exhausted her. The opera house was a small building, not much larger than St. Timothy of the Bayou Catholic Church, across the grassy town square, where generations of her family had been baptized and married and, in the fullness of time, buried in the cemetery behind the church.

Alexandre was there, waiting for her.

Titus opened the heavy carved door and she stepped into the lobby. It needed paint, she could see that even in the watery light. And the scars from Yankee boots on the wide plank floors had never been repaired. The Lesatzes were good managers, but she couldn't provide them with the resources Alexandre and his family had enjoyed before the War of Northern Aggression, as she still thought of the conflict that had torn apart the country of her birth.

Once more Titus preceded her as she entered the auditorium with its faded velvet seats, removed and hidden during the war, on either side of a central aisle leading to the stage. She was glad she had been able to hang on to the opera house through the lean years. She looked up at the two small gilded boxes on either side of the stage, reached by narrow balconies connected to matching staircases situated to the right and left of the doors.

"My *maman* will not sit with hoi polloi," Alexandre had laughed when Amelie, her practical Acadian soul shocked at the expense, had protested the extravagance of their construction. And he had been right. The few times Josephine Valois had deigned to attend one of her daughter-in-law's performances, for friends and family, never the public, she had indeed sat in the small gilt chairs that graced the boxes, in regal and solitary splendor.

It hadn't mattered to Amelie, then. Not Josephine's coldness, not her own family's disappointment that she had married away from their close-knit Acadian community. Nothing else had mattered when she had Alexandre. Even the ache of no babies of her own was kept at bay when he was at her side.

But then war had come. The invading Yankees had turned the opera house into a hospital, commandeering the plantation house for their headquarters, displacing the womenfolk to La Petite Maison, a cypress cottage on the Bayou Teche. Amelie had not minded returning to the simpler life she'd known as a girl, but the shock and humiliation had nearly killed Josephine Valois.

The war was almost over when word came that Alexandre was dead, and with that devastating news, for Amelie, everything changed. Her in-laws resented her, blamed her for Alexandre's death because she had given him no sons, no reason to stay out of the conflict. Her own parents were broken by the loss of their farm in the aftermath of the war. Her brothers had died in the fighting; her sister, also left widowed, had three young children to raise alone. When, at the urging of distant cousins, they all decided to move to Acadie—Nova Scotia, as it was called in the newly formed country of Canada—Amelie went, too.

Later, after they had lost the plantation, Josephine and Henri Valois and their surviving son and daughter had followed. The years passed, her family prospered once more. Amelie took comfort in her nieces and nephews and returned to Indigo from time to time when she could bear to be parted from her love no longer. Lately the longing had been even stronger, urging her to undertake a winter journey her relatives and her doctor all cautioned against.

Her breathing was still labored and shallow. She didn't attempt to mount the stage. Instead she handed the pale-cream camellia that she had kept sheltered near her heart to Titus. "Will you put this on the stage for me, old friend?"

"Of course, Miss Amelie. My, this is a pretty one. Just like the ones Mr. Alexandre always gave you to wear in your hair before you sang."

"Yes, Titus." She watched him walk forward to place her token to a lost love on the stage. In her mind she could hear all the wonderful music that had been performed in this building in those happier times: Beethoven and Bach and Mozart, traditional Acadian ballads, classic French opera, the village children singing Christmas carols, even, daringly, Negro spirituals. She and Alexandre had loved them all.

As she still loved him. "Let's go, Titus," she said, warmed and strengthened by her memories. "I want to visit my husband's grave before darkness falls."

"Yes, Miss Amelie, we'll do just that. I expect Mr. Alexandre, he'll be right glad to see you again." Once more he offered his arm, leading her out of her opera house for the last time.

CHAPTER ONE

Indigo, Louisiana, present day

"HURRY, CECILY," Yvonne Valois cautioned her daughter in the Cajun French that was her first language. "We don't have all day for this." From her seat at the late Maude Picard's kitchen table, she could see the comings and goings of the three other women who moved around the century-old shotgun-style house.

"Mother, lower your voice—you're in a house of death," Cecily Boudreaux admonished without much hope of being attended to. She pulled out yet another drawer stuffed full of gadgets and gizmos and odd bits and pieces of mismatched silver. Her mother had spent seventy-five years ordering people around in that tone of voice. She wasn't going to stop today just because her grandson, Indigo's Chief of Police, had found her old friend slumped over dead in her living room.

"Why not speak as I wish? Maude's beyond caring and Marie's as lazy as she can hold together. She'll be all day if I don't get her attention."

"Shh, she'll hear you and it *will* take the rest of the afternoon to coax her out of her pout."

Yvonne firmed her lips but said no more as Marie Lesatz chose that moment to enter the room. She was a small-boned woman with short dark hair and dark eyes, several years past her fiftieth birthday.

"Will this do?" The tall, black woman following Marie moved forward unhurriedly. At sixty-five Estelle Jefferson was a decade older than Cecily and Marie. She and her husband Willis owned the Blue Moon Diner, and served the best mix of Cajun and Creole favorites for miles around. She held up a navy-blue flowered dress. "I always liked Maude in this dress."

"It's the only halfway decent thing in her closet." Marie's tone was acid as she dropped onto the ladder-back chair beside Yvonne.

Yvonne switched to English now that she and Cecily were no longer alone. Marie's Cajun was limited and Estelle spoke no French at all. "I always thought she looked better in her gray silk."

"If you're not satisfied with the dress I picked out, you go look for the gray silk. I'm not rooting through a dead woman's closet anymore. Especially that one." Marie gestured over her shoulder toward Maude's bedroom. "It's stuffed full of clothes. Maude never threw anything away, you know that."

You certainly ought to know about stuffed closets, Cecily thought with a spurt of annoyance. Marie owned more clothes than any other woman in Indigo, and kept buying them every chance she got whether she could afford them or not.

Marie caught her eye, obviously reading her thoughts, and pushed up her chin in defiance. Marie had been Cecily's childhood friend, but Marie was also her son's ex-mother-in-law, and that's where the problem lay. Indigo was too small a town for Cecily and Marie to be at each other's throats. Cecily swallowed her pique. "The navy will do just fine," she said.

"I even went through her underwear drawer, God forgive me." Marie made the sign of the cross. "Nothing there is fit for a *vendre de maison*. And no, I didn't come across any keys," she added before Cecily could ask.

"There's far too much stuff here for a garage sale," Yvonne decreed. Sophie Clarkson will have to call in an auctioneer. Anyway, we're not responsible for selling off Maude's possessions. That's for Sophie to decide. She's the heir. But Maude did let things go these last few years. What a mess." All four women looked around as though they could see through walls into the other small, overcrowded rooms, stuffed with antiques, knickknacks and *fatras,* just plain junk.

Maude Picard, owner of Past Perfect antique shop, had been their friend and the de facto leader of their group. *Smuggling ring*, Cecily corrected herself with a wince. Her mother and the others weren't just the La-gniappe Ladies, who met a couple of times a month to play cards or go out to dinner—a kind of homegrown version of the Red Hat Ladies whose name meant "a little something extra." The Lagniappe Ladies were criminals, plain and simple. And their latest shipment of illegal prescription drugs from Canada was locked up somewhere in Maude's shop.

"I've never seen so much junk in my life," Estelle agreed as she laid the blue dress over the back of a chair.

"I'm going back for shoes and her under things. It's not right she should meet the Almighty not wearing her underwear. And then I need to get on home. Willis wasn't feeling too well when I left. He took a pain pill but I want him off his feet and he won't do that if I'm not there to hound him." Willis Jefferson had been diagnosed with lung cancer two years earlier. He was taking an experimental anti-cancer drug that was prohibitively expensive and difficult to obtain—and his next dose was sitting beyond reach in the opera house along with all the rest of their shipment.

"You go ahead and leave any time you want," Yvonne said. "What about her jewelry, Marie? What did you pick?"

"I found these on top of her dresser." She dropped a pearl necklace and matching earrings into Yvonne's outstretched hand. "I'm not going through her jewelry box and then have that snooty goddaughter of hers show up from Houston and accuse us all of swiping something." She folded her arms across her chest. Marie had gone from frowning to pouting, just as Cecily had predicted. "And I think she'd be happier in her housecoat and slippers," she muttered under her breath.

Yvonne gave Marie a hard look. "We're not laying her to rest in her robe and slippers like swamp trash. The pearls will do fine."

Before the conversation could deteriorate further, Cecily spied a wooden cheese box on top of Maude's old round-shouldered Frigidaire and lifted it gingerly down. Two sets of keys glinted back at her. She held her breath. Were they the ones they'd been searching for? "Mama, look." She held them up. "Do you suppose?"

"They don't look like deadbolt keys to me," Marie said before Yvonne could respond, squinting to bring the keys into focus. "They look more like lockbox keys, or some such."

"I'm afraid she's right. You'd better leave them where they are. Maude may have left instructions about them for Sophie, although I doubt it, as forgetful as she's been the last few months." Yvonne rose heavily from the chair. She looked every day of her age this morning. Maude Picard had been her friend for many years. Although her health had been failing slowly, her sudden death had come as a shock to all of them, but especially to Yvonne.

"Alain found her slumped in the chair by the door," Cecily mused. "She was obviously leaving to open the shop when she felt the stroke coming on."

"Then her keys to both the house and the store were most likely in her purse and are still there," Yvonne suggested.

"Alain took her purse," Marie said. She was on the Indigo emergency squad and had responded to the 911 call. It was Marie who had informed the other Lagniappe Ladies of the sad event. "He'll keep everything at the jail until Sophie arrives, I bet. We'll have to think of some other way to get into Past Perfect."

Cecily could feel a headache starting to gather behind her eyes. She wanted to get this sad task over with so she could sit down and put her feet up for twenty minutes before Guy and Dana got home from school and started begging for snacks and whining about doing homework. She loved Alain and his children, loved having them live with her to keep her from rattling around in her big old house. But some days she just wanted to be alone for a while. "Outside of breaking and entering, I don't know how we'll manage to get our hands on them."

Yvonne gave a short, sharp nod. "If that's what it takes to get our property back without Alain knowing about it, then that's what we'll do."

ALAIN BOUDREAUX cruised by Maude Picard's place at a slow crawl. It was a few minutes past one o'clock and both his mother's and ex-mother-in-law's cars were still parked in the crushed-shell driveway that paralleled the long, narrow house. Tidying up, he supposed, cleaning perishables out of the fridge, laundering sheets for the guest room, sweeping, dusting a little. It was the kind of thing people did for each other in a place like Indigo. Especially when the dearly departed had no family of her own, as in Maude's case. Except for her goddaughter, of course. Sophie Clarkson. Alain tried to remember the last time he'd seen her. Had to be four, maybe even five years back.

A fleeting image of a pretty young girl darted into his thoughts. Sophie as she'd been the summer he'd turned nineteen and she'd come to spend a few weeks with Maude: blue-gray eyes, softly curling blond hair, a smile that started out slow and sweet then turned into heat and flame. He'd fallen head over heels in love with her that summer but it hadn't lasted. Couldn't last. They were from two different worlds. His roots were planted deep in the rich bayou soil of Indigo Parish. She was Houston oil money, trust-fund/country-club rich. He'd broken their relationship off shortly after she went off to college, and though she'd been upset, he'd known it was the right thing to do. They'd hardly seen each other since, except for the summer before his daughter, Dana, was born. Then, for one short week, they'd been something more. And all hell had broken loose.

Dredging up memories of Sophie Clarkson wasn't going to do anything but rile him up so he changed the focus of his thoughts. He'd better stop and see if everything was all right with the Lagniappe Ladies. Maude was the first of their group to die. It had to be upsetting for them, especially his *mamère*, who had been Maude's best friend for as long as he could remember.

He pulled the three-year-old Ford Explorer to the curb in front of Maude's house. The town council had scored the SUV from a federal grant that funneled drug dealers' confiscated vehicles to rural police departments. It was a sweet ride, with all the bells and whistles, and sure beat the road-weary sedan he'd been driving for the past two years since he became Indigo's Chief of Police, head of its eight-man department— three full-time officers and five part-timers who filled in on weekends and holidays.

Most of the time his small force was more than adequate for the problems he faced in a town the size of Indigo: animal calls, public intoxication, more domestic violence than he'd like and once in a while an old-timer out in the boonies selling a little too much moonshine from his homemade still. But not a lot of drugs, at least not any more than anywhere else these days, and damned near no violent crime at all. He liked that. Indigo was only a couple of hours' driving time from New Orleans, but it was a world away from the nonstop crime and violence he'd experienced in his five years on the New Orleans PD, and he was glad of it.

Alain unfolded his six-foot frame from the driver's seat and grabbed his Stetson, settling it on his head to keep off the rain. He wiped his feet on the mat on the narrow front porch, knocked, then opened the door and walked into the living room where he'd found Maude sitting peacefully in her favorite chair that morning, her handbag in her hands, her eyes closed as though she was just taking a bit of a catnap before leaving for work. But she hadn't been napping. She was dead. He'd known it the moment he'd touched her hand.

Stroke, most likely, Dr. Landry had said when he arrived from his office three doors down from the Savoy Funeral Home on the other side of the main drag, known officially as the River Road. He'd been treating Maude for high blood pressure and diabetes for the past twenty-five years and warning her for nearly as long to quit smoking and start taking better care of herself. Good old Mick Landry, Alain thought gratefully. He'd been tending to the births and deaths, and all the aches and pains in between, of Indigo's residents for more than half a century. He didn't get up in the middle of the night to bring babies into the world anymore, the way he had in the old days, but he was there for the dying. He'd signed the death certificate on the spot, saving Alain a lot of headaches dealing with the parish coroner and all the extra paperwork an unattended death entailed.

"Mama, *Mamère,* are you still here?" he asked in Cajun.

"In the kitchen," his mother called back. "We're just finishing up."

"The house is as ready for Sophie Clarkson as we can make it," his grandmother said in lieu of a greeting, angling her cheek for a kiss. Her hair was soft and white as dandelion fluff, and her skin pale as cream. His mother and sisters had the same soft, white skin and dark abundant hair that would turn snow-white with age, acquired from their Acadian ancestors. He had the warmer skin tones and chestnut-colored hair of a hard-drinking, silver-tongued, Irish great-grandfather who had sweet-talked his way onto a branch of the Boudreaux family tree. "You're all wet, *cher,*" Yvonne scolded, smiling to take the sting from her words.

"It's raining, *Mamère.* And it's cold. Big storm from up north coming this way."

"I know. I feel it in my bones."

His mother finished taking dishes from a rack and putting them in the old pine cabinets. She pushed back the heavy braid she'd worn her hair in for as long as he remembered, and closed the silverware drawer with a snap. "*Fini,*" she said with satisfaction, giving him a quick pat on the cheek. "Hello, *cher.*"

"Looks good, Mama." He liked this house. He wondered what would happen to it now that Maude was gone. The shotgun style was eminently suitable for the hot Louisiana summers. It had a lot of potential and he was good with his hands. He'd been thinking about getting a house of his own lately. He and the kids had been living with his mom for going on four years now, ever since they'd moved back to Indigo, and he and Casey Jo had called it quits for good. It was time they had a place of their own.

He knew Cecily wouldn't like the idea of rattling around in the big old two-story on Lafayette Street by herself, but it was time for a change. And maybe if he and the kids were gone, she'd find a man for herself. After all, his dad had died more than fifteen years ago. Dead in a logging accident at forty-five. The Valois were long-lived. His mother had too many good years ahead of her to spend them alone.

"Alain, it's you. I thought I heard a car drive up." His ex-mother-in-law appeared in his line of sight. She carried a spray bottle of bathroom cleaner and a couple of cleaning rags. As usual she was dressed too young for her age in tight jeans and a tank top, her makeup too bright, her improbably black hair curled and fluffed within an inch of its life.

"Hello, Marie. If everything's under control here, I'll get back to my patrol."

"Don't run off, Alain. I want to talk to you." Marie turned to Yvonne. "The bathroom's finished. Where do you want this stuff?"

"I'll put it away." Cecily took the cleaning supplies and disappeared into the utility room at the far side of the kitchen.

"How about if I stop by your place after supper?" He knew he was going to have to hear Marie out sooner or later. But he preferred later.

Marie dismissed his suggestion with a wave of her hand. "I've got a date for supper," she said with a lift of her penciled eyebrows. "This won't take long. I talked to Casey Jo last night. She told me she's been leaving messages for you all week."

"I haven't had a chance to get back to her. Hank Lassiter's off with a bad back. I've been pulling double shifts, you know that."

"I also know my daughter. When she's got a bee in her bonnet, it's hard to get her mind on something else."

"What is it this time?" he asked wearily. If it involved money he was going to say no. Casey Jo didn't contribute one red cent to raising their kids. She spent everything she made on herself, a habit she'd learned at her mama's knee, but it didn't stop her from trying to get money out of him whenever she ran short.

"She wants to take Guy and Dana to Disney World on their semester break."

"Disney World? That's a pretty pricey trip."

"She wants to make it up to them for not being able to get them much for Christmas," Marie said, biting her lower lip.

"She didn't get them much for Christmas because she spent all her money on botox injections." He did his best to keep the disgust he felt at that particular episode from his voice. Marie did what she could for him and the kids. She tended bar at a place out on the highway called the Ragin' Cajun most nights, but she was always there if he needed her to take the kids to school, or drop off forgotten homework or lunch boxes when his mom was working as a nurse at the hospital in Lafayette.

"You know how badly she wanted that spot on *American Idol*. Her agent told her—"

"She's thirty-four years old, Marie. Long past time to give up on big dreams and settle down to real life."

"But she's got talent—"

"So do thousands of other women."

Marie veered away from any more comments about Casey Jo's lifestyle. "I told her not to breathe a word to the kids until she'd okayed the trip with you."

Once more Alain swallowed his irritation. His mother-in-law was awkwardly placed, caught in the middle of a bad situation. She loved Guy and Dana, but she loved her daughter, too. "Thanks, Marie. I appreciate you not saying anything until after you'd talked to me. I don't want to get their hopes up again. Especially Dana's. Casey Jo's disappointed her too many times."

"I told her Guy probably wouldn't go," Yvonne broke in, having kept her silence as long as she cared to. "He is too important to the basketball team for the coach to allow him to take a week off in the middle of the season."

"I'll call her as soon as I get a minute," Alain promised, forestalling his grandmother's next remark before her sharp tongue reduced Marie to tears.

Cecily walked back into the room, shrugging into a heavy cotton sweater as she spoke. She was wearing jeans and a turtleneck that were nowhere near as tight or low-cut as Marie's clothes, and in Alain's opinion she looked about ten years younger than the other woman. "Sophie Clarkson phoned an hour or so ago. She's driving in from Houston and should arrive around two o'clock tomorrow. That's when the wake will start."

"I imagine she's never attended a wake," Marie muttered. "I mean, her not being Catholic and all."

"I have no idea if she's been to a wake or not." Alain picked up his Stetson and set it on his head. No way was he going to let his ex-mother-in-law draw him into a conversation about the woman Casey Jo insisted had broken up their marriage. "I've got to get back on patrol."

"I've got a roast in the oven for supper," his mother reminded him.

"Keep a plate warm for me, will you? I've got a ton of paperwork to fill out before I call it a day."

"Try not to be too late."

"I'll do my best. Tell Dana I'll be home in time to tuck her in." At seven, his daughter was at the age where she was growing up in a lot of ways, but still, he thought thankfully, she was daddy's little girl in others. Tucking her in at night was one of the high points of his day. Which went a long way in explaining why he didn't have much of a social life.

He started toward the front door but stopped at the sound of his grandmother's voice. "Alain. We've done the best we can with this place but it still needs a lot of work. Do you know where Maude's keys might be? If we have them we could come back and finish up tomorrow."

He heard his mother suck in her breath and turned

to look at her. Her eyes slid past his and she whirled around to wipe an already spotless sink.

"The door was open when I found her, but I imagine the keys are in her purse. That's one of the things I have to do this afternoon—inventory Maude's effects." He glanced around. His mother and grandmother and the others had been working for most of the day to make Maude's house welcoming for a woman who hadn't spent more than ten days in Indigo in the last five years. That was enough as far as he was concerned. "The house looks fine." He cleared his throat of the residue of old anger that had roughened his words. "I don't think you need to do anything else. With an upscale place like La Petite Maison right down the road. I'd be surprised if Sophie Clarkson spends a single night under this roof."

CHAPTER TWO

"I WANT TO EXTEND my most sincere sympathy, Miss Sophie," the stooped, white-haired man said, taking Sophie's hand between his knobby, arthritic fingers. "I'm Maurice Renaurd. I owned the hardware here for many years. Maude and I served on the library board together. She was a good woman. She'll be missed."

"Thank you," Sophie said, smiling. "I'll miss her, too." She spoke with sincerity and an underlying remorse. She was overwhelmed by the number of people who had already filed through the viewing room of the Savoy Funeral Home, and it was barely six o'clock in the evening. The wake had only just begun.

She had neglected her godmother these past few years and she was sorry for it. But she had been so busy, and Maude had kept insisting that she was fine, that there was no reason to come more often than her usual summer weekend and Christmas week visit. But obviously there had been reason and Sophie knew she would always regret that she hadn't spent that extra time with her godmother.

She sighed. It seemed the older she got, the more things there were to regret in her life. She looked around, wondering when one of her earliest and most costly mistakes, at least in terms of heartache, would walk through the door. She hadn't seen Alain Boudreaux in several years. It had been almost twice that long since she'd exchanged private words with him.

"Do you have everything you need?" Marjolaine Savoy's smile was practiced but genuine as she came to stand beside Sophie near the casket. She was a tall woman with a head of dark brown hair that she wore in a French braid down her back. Marjolaine was the director of the Savoy Funeral Home, the third generation of her family to be involved in the business, according to the brochure Sophie had glanced through during a lull in the visitation.

"I'm fine, thanks. A little thirsty, though." Sophie couldn't help letting her gaze wander to the dozen or so people grouped around a big marble-topped table drinking punch and sweet tea and eating cookies. She'd driven all the way from Houston, almost five hours, with only one stop for gas and no food, and she was beginning to feel the effects of the long day.

"You need a break," Marjolaine urged. "It's my job to make sure the mourners don't overdo. Come along with me. There's no one in line to pay their respects at the moment, and if someone does come in, you can see them through the doorway." She was already leading Sophie into the smaller room with a firm but gentle hand under her elbow. "There're cookies on the table but I can get you a sandwich if you need something a little more substantial."

"Could you?" Sophie asked, giving up the pretense

of not needing a break. "I haven't eaten since breakfast, and I have the terrible feeling if I don't get something inside me soon, my stomach is going to start protesting long and loud." She managed a smile of her own. "I don't want to offend any of Aunt Maude's friends."

"It'll only take a moment. Is ham and cheese okay?"

"Ham and cheese sounds wonderful. Are you sure it isn't a problem?"

"No problem. It's going to be a long night. But a sandwich should hold you over until they set out the buffet around midnight."

Sophie opened her eyes a little wider. "I'd forgotten a wake lasts all night. I…I've never been to one before." She'd never had to spend much time in funeral homes, but she knew from the rare occasions she'd accompanied her grandmother to pay her respects to friends and business acquaintances, the sedate viewings lasted only until nine or so in the evening. They didn't go on all night with friends bringing in food and drinks, music playing and talk of happier times, as they often did in Cajun country.

"You don't have to stay all night if you don't want to," Marjolaine assured her, her blue eyes fixed on Sophie's face. "One or another of the Lagniappe Ladies will always be here. It will be a quiet one, I imagine, since there's no family but yourself."

"My parents are flying in for the funeral tomorrow, and my grandmother would have come with me but she's in Australia," Sophie explained. "My grandfather gave her the trip as a gift for her eightieth birthday, and she feels very badly that she can't be here." Darlene

Clarkson and Maude Picard had been friends from the first day they met at college at the end of the Second World War. It was Darlene who had prevailed on Sophie's parents to allow Maude to be her godmother. Sophie's mother had been particularly pleased she'd acceded to her mother's request when Maude made Sophie her heir on her twenty-first birthday.

"You can go to Maude's house to rest if you get too tired," Marjolaine said.

"No. I'll stay. Besides, I don't have a key to the house. You don't know who took charge of her things, do you?"

"We have nothing here, if that's what you're asking. Alain Boudreaux found her body. He's probably taken custody of her personal possessions for you. He's Chief of Police now, you know."

Sophie felt her facial muscles tense slightly but hoped it didn't show in her expression. "I'd forgotten," she fibbed. "But now that you mention it, I recall *Nanan* Maude telling me about his promotion to chief."

Marjolaine's eyes narrowed slightly. Sophie could almost see her mind sifting through her memories, sorting out the bits and pieces that pertained to Sophie and Alain Boudreaux. "He's been back in Indigo for three—no, four years. Since right after his divorce from Casey Jo became final."

"I know about the divorce." Sophie hoped her voice sounded normal, interested but not *too* interested. Marjolaine might not even remember she and Alain had been an item the summer after her high-school graduation. Fifteen years was a long time, after all. And she prayed that for both their sakes, but mostly for Alain's, no one had learned about the other short, but intense relationship they'd shared after she'd run to Maude for comfort when her marriage collapsed. It was a reconciliation that had ended almost before it began, when Casey Jo had found Sophie in Alain's arms,

Sophie still burned with embarrassment whenever she thought of that horrible scene. She and Alain hadn't committed adultery as Casey Jo accused, not physically, but they might as well have. Since then they had never been alone, had barely spoken to each other, and, over the last few years, she hadn't done much more than catch a glimpse of him across the town square during her infrequent visits.

"Divorced. Going on five years now. Casey Jo, she's off dealing blackjack in a Mississippi casino and trying out for *American Idol*. Can you believe that?" Marjolaine grinned.

"I remember she was very pretty." Night-black hair, long, long legs and model-thin. No wonder Alain had fallen so hard for her after he and Sophie broke up. And he'd gotten her pregnant almost the first time he went out with her, if the gossip one of her old summer friends had passed along to her was right. And it must have been, because Alain and Casey Jo's son, Guy, was fifteen years old and the star center on the high-school basketball team. Another small fact of Alain's life that her traitorous mind had filed away and refused to forget. Her stomach growled loudly enough for Marjolaine to hear.

"I'll get you that sandwich," she said. She walked

to the back of the room and disappeared through a set of swinging doors into what Sophie supposed was the kitchen.

She turned toward one of the small round tables set up in the room, but before she could take a seat, another elderly man approached her. "Miss Sophie, I'm Hugh Prejean. I'm the town librarian. Maude was on the library board. She was one of our staunchest supporters. She will be missed." The man, dressed in an old-fashioned white linen suit, holding a white fedora in his hands, looked like something out of a Faulkner novel. He sounded like one of Faulkner's characters, too, his vowels soft and rounded, his words and gestures as formal as their surroundings.

Sophie set her punch cup down on the table and shook his hand. "Thank you, Mr. Prejean. I know how much Maude loved books. She was very proud of Indigo's library."

"She also worked with me on the history of the Valois Opera House, did you know that?"

"Yes, I do."

He angled his body so that he could see the flower-bedecked walnut casket from where they stood. "We spent many hours researching the history of the building. The town is looking to restore it to its former glory, you know, Miss Sophie. That is, if we can get title to the building."

"I do know the owner is Canadian," Sophie said. Everyone who had any connection at all to Indigo knew that much about the opera house. It had been built originally by an aristocratic—and distant—ancestor of

Alain Boudreaux's, on his mother's side, for his talented and beautiful young Cajun bride, then passed to Canadian relatives after her death. Maude had leased the building for her business for years, always dealing with a lawyer from New Orleans when negotiations or repairs were necessary.

"Do you anticipate reopening Past Perfect anytime soon, Miss Sophie?" Hugh asked. "Meaning no disrespect to her memory, but Maude and I were in the middle of authenticating an early twentieth-century appearance here of Miss Lillian Russell. It would be a draw for tourists, you know. And it would also be beneficial in our quest to get the opera house listed on the state registry of historical sites. All our research material is filed away in her office, not to mention the old records themselves, still up in the attic." He looked out the window behind them, although Sophie knew he could see nothing but their reflections. He shook his head, making little tsking noises with his tongue. "All this rain. The roof isn't in good repair although we do our best. Maude intended to speak to the lawyer about it again right soon."

"I don't know about reopening the business, Mr. Prejean," Sophie said honestly. She hadn't thought that far ahead. After all, her godmother had been dead less than two days. "I...I know very little about antiques." It was true she had loved working for Maude during her teenage years, and had learned to appreciate the quality of the craftsmanship and artistry of the pieces Maude treasured and hated to part with; as well as the whimsy and appeal of the not-so-valuable collectibles that

Maude confessed formed a bigger percentage of her yearly profits than one would suspect. But her parents hadn't raised Sophie to run a small-town antique shop, and when she graduated from Bard College, her mother's alma mater, she had returned to Houston and entered the family business as a fund-raising consultant to several small universities and hospitals.

"Oh dear, but yes, I see that might be a problem." Hugh's long face drooped with disappointment.

"However, I'll certainly inform you as soon as Chief Boudreaux turns Maude's keys over to me so that you may retrieve your reference materials and take a look at the roof." She smiled and lifted her hand palm up. "You see, I have no way to get into the opera house, or my godmother's home for that matter, until he releases her effects to me. I hope you understand."

His hangdog expression cleared. He gave her a thin-lipped but genuine smile that crinkled his eyes. "Of course, I should have realized that would be the case. I will wait to hear from you, then. And in the meantime, if there's any way I can be of service to you, do not hesitate to call on me."

"How kind of you," Sophie said, and she meant it.

Marjolaine appeared at her elbow carrying a china plate with a ham and cheese sandwich and a sprig of green grapes as the old man walked away. "Here's your sandwich." Sophie took the plate with a grateful smile. "I see you met Hugh Prejean. He's a dear old soul. Maude and I were helping him research the opera house records. We're hoping we can come up with enough facts and figures to get it on the state historical register."

"Mr. Prejean was just explaining all that to me."

"I hope you'll allow us to keep digging through the attic. Most of the old records are still stored up there and the roof is none too good. We'd like to get them someplace safer before they deteriorate any further."

"I already promised him I would let him know as soon as I have possession of the keys to the opera house."

"Thanks, I appreciate that, too."

"No problem." What she omitted telling Marjolaine was that while she certainly meant what she said, she also didn't intend to confront Alain Boudreaux one minute sooner than she absolutely had to.

"THERE SHE IS." Marie looked though the narrow opening of the partially closed pocket doors that shielded Maude's mourners from drafts of wet January air. "She's sitting at that little table by the window talking to Marjolaine."

They were huddled in the big, high-ceilinged foyer of the funeral home, Cecily, Yvonne and Marie, each holding a casserole dish and dripping water onto the polished wood floor. "Don't trip, Mama," Cecily cautioned. "This floor is like glass."

"I wonder how Marjolaine gets it to shine like that?" Marie mused, sliding the open toe of her stiletto heels over the glossy wood. Cecily looked down at her own sensible black, two-inch pumps.

"I have no idea and I'm not asking her."

"Good evening, ladies. You'll be wanting to take those dishes into the kitchen, I imagine." Henry Roy, the undertaker who worked for Marjolaine, glided through the pocket doors separating the foyer from the viewing room and slid them shut behind him with the ease of many years' practice, shutting off their view of the principal mourner. "But first let me take your coats, won't you."

Once he'd divested the women of their coats and umbrellas, Henry opened a door beneath the sweep of the main staircase and ushered them down a narrow hallway to the kitchen. "*Merci,* Henry, we know our way around," Yvonne said as the undertaker pushed open the swinging door into the kitchen. "You can go back to the front." Henry and Yvonne were old allies in the rituals of small-town death. With a nod he retreated down the dark, narrow hall.

"This place always gives me the willies," Marie complained when they were alone again.

"It's just a kitchen," Cecily sniffed.

"A funeral home kitchen." She shuddered and folded her hands beneath her breasts. "The whole house is creepy."

Footsteps echoed in the hallway. "Hush," Yvonne warned.

"Hello, Yvonne, Cecily, Marie." Marjolaine entered the room just as Yvonne slid the last casserole into the big oven. "Henry told me you'd arrived. I see you have everything you need."

"Gabriel has everything laid out for us," Cecily said, patting the braided bun that hung heavily on the back of her neck. Marjolaine had long, straight hair the same as she did, but she always wore hers in an intricate French braid that Cecily had never had the patience to learn how to produce.

"He's a good boy," Yvonne approved.

"He tries hard." Marjolaine smiled, but her eyes were troubled as they usually were when her mentally challenged younger brother was the topic of conversation. "The tables are set up in the Ladies' Parlor. I'll have Gabriel start the coffee as soon as Father Joe finishes the prayer service."

"*Bon.*"

Just then Estelle Jefferson and Helen Simone, the sixth and newest member of the Lagniappe Ladies, came through the back door of the kitchen, both laden with casserole dishes in padded baskets. "Sorry we're late," Estelle said.

"How's Willis doing today?" Marjolaine asked.

"Fair to middlin'," Estelle responded.

"He'll feel better when the weather breaks." Marjolaine set the plate and glass she'd carried into the kitchen with her in the big double sink and exited the room, leaving the Lagniappe Ladies alone.

Estelle and Helen placed their casseroles in the oven alongside the others and turned to Yvonne. "Are we ready?" she asked.

Yvonne nodded, pulling her rosary out of her pocket. "Yes," she said. "Let's go say *au revoir* to Maude, and then we'll figure out how we're going to sweet-talk Sophie Clarkson into letting us inside the opera house without my grandson finding out what we're up to."

Marie didn't budge from where she was standing. "I say after the funeral we just walk up to her and ask for the key to get our stuff out of the shop. I mean, it's not like we're smuggling heroin or something like that. We paid for it. We have receipts and everything."

"But we still smuggled it into the country," Helen pointed out, biting her lip. "It's against the law to bring prescription drugs over the border and you know it." Helen was a timid woman and their activities had never set well with her. "Especially one like Willis's that's banned in the States."

"Banned is right," Cecily hissed. "Why do you think we've been doing it like this for the past two years?"

"I was never so frightened in my life as when I got that letter from the government people saying they'd confiscated Willis's pills and we could be arrested if we tried ordering them from Canada again," Estelle murmured.

Cecily lowered her voice to a whisper, but even then it vibrated with emotion. "We have to get our shipment out of the opera house and that's all there is to it. It's not just the six of us. There's another dozen people waiting for their medications, remember." She wasn't ashamed of what they were doing, but she was worried about what might happen to all of them, and to Alain, if they were caught. "But we've got to be smart about this. We can't just walk up to Sophie Clarkson and ask straight out for the shipment unless—"

"Unless what?" Marie demanded.

Cecily gave up; she couldn't let Willis and the others down. "Unless we absolutely have to."

CHAPTER THREE

SOPHIE SMOTHERED a yawn behind her hand. The music playing on the funeral home's PA system, a mixture of Cajun ballads and folk tunes instead of the somber classical or religious orchestrations she'd expected, wasn't loud enough or lively enough to keep her awake. It was almost midnight but there were about twenty people scattered throughout the viewing and refreshment rooms, eating, drinking, talking and even laughing softly now and then. Someone, it seemed, was always at her side, everyone friendly and solicitous, trying hard to include her in their conversations. But her connection to Indigo had been tenuous at best the last several years and she found herself only truly engaged when someone was speaking of Maude.

Sophie had eaten her fill of Blue Moon Diner gumbo and Yvonne Valois's sweet potato pie when the buffet was set out an hour ago, and had drunk what seemed like a gallon of coffee, but the intake of sugar and caffeine hadn't helped. She was so tired she could barely keep her eyes open. And at the moment she felt like kicking herself for not accepting Marjolaine's invitation to go upstairs and take a short nap. How would she ever make it through the entire night and half the next day without falling asleep on her feet?

"You know there's no rule that says you have to be here every minute," a masculine voice said from behind her.

Sophie spun around. The man now standing before her was young, a quality which had been in short supply that evening. He was probably in his late twenties, broad-shouldered, blond and blue-eyed. When he smiled, Sophie's breath caught in her throat for a moment or two. He was so handsome it was an absolute sin.

He held out his hand and Sophie took it automatically. "Ms. Clarkson, my name's Luc Carter." He wasn't a native of Indigo, she could tell that right away. His vowels were clipped, his words too precise. She guessed he had grown up in the north, or possibly out west. "I moved to the area about ten months ago. I didn't know Maude Picard as well as the others here, but we were becoming friends. My condolences."

"Thank you, Mr. Carter." Sophie had recovered her breath and her poise.

Luc Carter smiled and released her hand. "I meant it when I said protocol doesn't demand you stay here all night. You look beat."

"That bad?" she asked. She restrained herself from raising her hand to pat her hair. It was blond—naturally—shoulder-length, curly and flyaway, the bane of her existence.

He had the grace to look chagrined. "Sorry, I phrased that badly. I know you drove all the way from Houston today. It will be another long day tomorrow. No one expects you to be here every single moment in between. You should get some rest if you have the chance."

"As a matter of fact, Marjolaine offered me a bed upstairs, but—" This time it was her turn to stumble to a halt.

"But you don't exactly feel like napping in a funeral home, right?"

"I know it's silly, but you're right, I do feel that way. Unfortunately I have nowhere else to go." A little spurt of annoyance sharpened her words. "Alain Boudreaux has the keys to my godmother's house and he hasn't seen fit to show up here and give them to me yet tonight."

Luc angled his head a fraction. "Why don't you come home with me?" he asked.

"I beg your pardon?" Sophie hoped she didn't sound as shocked as she felt. Who was this guy?

He saw her confusion and smiled. "That's an invitation, not a proposition. Marjolaine can vouch for me. I run La Petite Maison. The Little Cottage," he explained when he saw her bewildered expression. "It's a bed-and-breakfast."

"I had no idea there was a bed-and-breakfast operating anywhere near Indigo," Sophie said, relaxing a little. She began to register the friendly smiles and waves of greeting directed toward Luc Carter and dismissed the unworthy thoughts of ax murderers and gigolos that had stampeded through her tired brain moments earlier. "My godmother never mentioned it."

"We're located not quite a mile out of town, on the

bayou road. I'm the manager, plumber, gardener and concierge, but the property is actually owned by my grandmother."

"Have I met her?" Sophie asked politely. Family connections were important in Indigo, one always inquired.

"I doubt it," Luc said a little abruptly, then softened the sharp words with a smile. "She's lived in New Orleans for decades, but La Petite Maison was the family's summer getaway many years ago."

"And you've always dreamed of running a hotel, right?"

His easy smile faltered for a moment. "Actually I've been in the hotel business for several years."

"Ah, but you always wanted to open a place of your own," Sophie amended.

"Something like that."

"You have a room available for the rest of the night, then?"

"Not just tonight. I've only been open a few weeks. I can accommodate you for as long as you wish to stay in Indigo. As a matter of fact, if you don't mind climbing an extra flight of stairs, you can have the attic suite. It has a whirlpool tub and a private bath. The other four rooms share."

"A Jacuzzi. That sounds like heaven." Her exhaustion was fast overcoming her guilt at leaving the wake.

"And the view from the balcony's not bad, either. It overlooks the gardens and the Bayou Teche. It's a little early for the gardens but I never get tired of watching the river roll by."

"Do you really think it's okay for me to leave?" Marjolaine had told her the same thing, but Sophie felt uncomfortable just walking away from Maude's wake. She looked around the room. Three of Maude's friends—the Lagniappe Ladies, Marjolaine had called them—were sitting on chairs to the left of the casket. Two of them were Alain's mother and Estelle Jefferson, whom Sophie had met earlier. The third was Alain's ex-mother-in-law, Marie Lesatz. If Sophie stayed, she would be expected to join them at their vigil.

And then there was Alain himself. She was coward enough to be happy to avoid seeing him at all if she could manage it. She turned back to Luc, willing a smile to her lips: "I would love to stay at La Petite Maison. Can you wait a moment while I get my coat?"

Five minutes later they were standing on the wide verandah of the funeral home. The rain was still coming down, cold and relentless. Fog rose from the low places in the rolling lawn that surrounded the building and wreathed the streetlight overhead. Sophie shivered. It wasn't as cold as it sometimes got in Houston, but the dampness crept into your bones if you lingered outside too long.

"Is your car nearby?" Luc asked her. He was holding the huge black umbrella that Marjolaine had pressed on Sophie when she'd sought out the funeral home manager to tell her of the change in plans. Marjolaine had seemed pleased with her decision, stating that she was looking forward to seeing the improvements Luc Carter had made to La Petite Maison, and laying to rest any last doubts Sophie had about driving off into the night with the handsome stranger.

"I'm parked in the church lot." She pointed across the street to St. Timothy's.

"If you give me your keys I'll bring your car around."

Sophie opened her mouth to assure him she could find her own way to the bed-and-breakfast when a big black SUV with a reflective Indigo Police Department decal rolled to a stop beside them. The door opened and Alain Boudreaux got out. Sophie would have known him anywhere, the tall lanky build, the easy athletic grace with which he moved, the way he tilted his head a little to the left when he walked. He was still in uniform, and aside from the plastic-covered gray Stetson on his head, dressed all in black—shirt, pants, shoes and leather bomber jacket. "Speak of the devil," Luc said quietly under his breath. "I believe it's Chief Boudreaux himself come to pay his respects to the dead."

"CARTER." Alain touched his fingers to the brim of his hat.

"Chief," Luc responded in a neutral tone. "Busy night?" he inquired pleasantly enough.

"Always is when it rains this hard. Some people just never get the hang of driving on wet roads." Alain turned his head slightly to bring the woman standing beside Indigo's newest citizen into view. "Hello, Sophie," he said. Her face was shadowed by the big black umbrella Carter held over both of them, but he didn't need to see the expression in her slanting, gray-blue eyes to know she was wary of him.

"Hello, Alain," she said in a polite, distantly friendly voice, as if he were only another of the near strangers who had already offered her condolences that night. He didn't attempt to shake her hand because he didn't quite trust himself to touch her. Would that old snap and sizzle of awareness still be there between them? Or was it gone, withered away with the passage of time and neglect? He wasn't prepared to find out just then.

She didn't offer her hand either, keeping both of them shoved deep into the pockets of her expensive-looking suede trench coat. She had belted it close around her slim waist, showing him she still had the kind of figure that stirred a man's blood.

"I'm sorry I couldn't get here earlier to pay my respects. There was an accident out on the highway. Three-car pileup, and the parish sheriff couldn't see his way clear to send a deputy this far south just for road-block patrol." That kind of neglect of Indigo and its environs was all too common an occurrence, and one of the reasons he was thinking of running for sheriff himself come the next election.

"You don't have to apologize for doing your job, Alain. I hope no one was seriously hurt." Her voice was softer this time.

"No fatalities," he said.

"I'm glad."

"I'm taking Ms. Clarkson to La Petite Maison so she can get a couple of hours rest," Carter inserted smoothly. Alain cut a glance at the younger man. He was dressed in a dark suit and white shirt open at the throat. The shirt was silk and the suit had a European cut and looked to be imported. He and Sophie made a striking couple. A remnant of his old insecurity stirred inside Alain, surprising him with its resurrection. It had been a long time since he'd felt he didn't measure up.

He turned his attention back to Sophie. "I was bringing you Maude's effects," he said, angling his head toward the SUV. "I meant to get them to you several hours before this. I'm sorry I didn't make it." Rain dripped off the brim of his hat and found its way down the collar of his coat. He hunched his shoulders slightly against the chill.

"Your duty comes first," Sophie said once more in that polite but distant tone that told him she didn't want any more to do with him than she had to.

"I can give you a lift to Maude's place if you don't want to make the drive out to the B&B." The offer came out of his mouth without his thinking of it. It was an automatic response, a learned behavior. She was unfamiliar with the area. It was late at night, raining hard. It was his duty as an officer of the law to make sure she didn't come to harm. Nothing more.

"La Petite Maison's only a mile out of town, but I was about to offer Ms. Clarkson a ride if she's too tired to drive her own car."

Again Alain turned his attention to the other man. It was the look in his eyes, he decided, something that told him the suit and the shirt and shoes might be expensive, but Luc Carter hadn't always been rolling in dough. And then there were the unanswered questions about his past. The trouble in New Orleans that had landed him in enough hot water to get him sentenced to probation for two years and exiled to a place like Indigo.

"What I'm too tired to do is stand here in the rain arguing about where to spend the night." Sophie's sharp words cut into his musings about Luc Carter's recent brush with the law. "I thank you both for your offers to drive me to my night's lodging, but I think I can manage to get to the B&B on my own. Chief Boudreaux, I'd appreciate it if you'd have my godmother's effects ready when I pull up." She gave him a look that even in the dim light was easy enough for Alain to read: she'd had a long day with another one looming before her and she had no intention of becoming the bone in a dog fight. She ducked out from under the sheltering umbrella and headed for her car.

"I think we've been put in our places," Luc said, watching her slim, straight back disappear into the shadow of St. Timothy's.

"Without a doubt." Alain kept his attention focused on the other man. Maybe it was time to dig a little deeper into Luc Carter's past. The B&B was owned by Celeste Robichaux, Luc's grandmother. Luc's father had been her son, Pierre, though Luc had chosen to go by his mother's maiden name for some reason. To the old-timers of Indigo, Celeste Robichaux was a well-known figure. But few people, except those such as Alain's own grandmother, to whom family ties and blood lines were all-important, knew that Celeste's daughter had married a man named Remy Marchand and now owned a hotel in New Orleans.

A hotel that had been in the news a lot a year or so ago.

"I can see the wheels turning in your head, Boudreaux," Luc said. "I haven't stepped one foot out of line or been as much as five minutes late meeting my parole officer since I got here."

"I know."

Carter raised an eyebrow. "Professional courtesy between the New Orleans PD and Indigo?"

"Something like that."

"No need to start hassling me just because I offered the lady a place to stay for the night. It's my job, remember."

"No hassle, Carter. Just doing *my* job. You were charged with felony theft, criminal mischief, fraud and conspiracy. Not exactly a ringing endorsement of your good citizenship. Sending a woman off alone with an accused felon wouldn't be fulfilling my obligation to serve and protect the citizens of Indigo, now would it?"

"Look, what I did back in New Orleans wasn't smart, but I've spent the last ten months working my fingers to the bone on the cottage to make restitution to the Marchands."

"Your family, you mean."

When Luc didn't say anything, Alain decided not to press the matter.

Luc's eyes glittered in the reflected light of the streetlamp. "I'm serving two years probation. After that, three more years of model citizenship will get me a clean record. It will sure as hell be easier to accomplish if the whole town doesn't know about me." A car engine purred to life in the church parking lot. Carter angled his head in that direction. "Here comes Ms. Clarkson. What am I supposed to tell her?"

Luc was right. He'd kept his nose clean since he'd come to Indigo and Alain had no good reason for giving him a hard time, other than the fact that he hadn't liked seeing him stand so close to Sophie under the big umbrella. He gave the other man a curt nod. "I'll get Maude's things for her while you bring your car around."

CHAPTER FOUR

THE DAY of the funeral was cool but sunny. The low dark clouds and cold rain that had persisted all through the night of Maude's wake had been blown away by the wind that sprang up just before dawn, allowing the few weary mourners who remained a glimpse of a glorious sunrise. By the time her godmother was laid to rest in the pink marble Picard vault in the cemetery behind St. Timothy's church, blue skies canopied the crowd of friends and townspeople who attended the service.

There had been tears at the funeral, but none at the luncheon that followed in the church hall. Like the dark clouds, the sadness was swept away by the happy memories of Maude's long, busy life. By the time Sophie had said her last goodbyes to the mourners, assured her parents it was okay for them to go back to Houston and leave her behind in Indigo, and driven back to the B&B, she was so tired she'd gone directly to bed and slept until noon the next day.

She'd awakened feeling rested physically, but reluctant to leave the B&B. She wished her grandmother could be with her. She didn't want to face sorting through Maude's possessions on her own. Now it was the middle of the afternoon and she still hadn't stirred herself to go into town but sat rocking on the wide front porch of La Petite Maison. She wrapped her sweater more tightly around her and set her chair gently swaying with her foot. She was honest enough to admit that some of her reluctance to leave the B&B resulted from the fear she would find more than a few unwanted memories of her long-ago summer romance with Alain Boudreaux lurking among Maude's things.

The screen door opened. "I brought tea and scones and muffins," Luc announced, offering her a teak tray covered with a vintage embroidered tea towel and set with green Depression glass and a silver teapot, covered with a second towel knotted around it as a cozy. "But I can take them back if you're not in the mood for tea right now."

"No. Please stay. A cup of tea sounds heavenly."

"I don't want to interrupt your reverie."

"My reverie was coming perilously close to turning into a nap," Sophie admitted. "It's so pleasant out here I'm tempted never to move again." The B&B was a wonderful place. An authentic, two-hundred-year-old raised Creole cottage built of native cypress timber with a cedar-shake roof. The guest rooms all recently remodeled, had access to the porches that ran the length of the building. Her tiny attic suite even had a small balcony of its own. In another month or two the yard would be a riot of blooming shrubs and spring flowers lining the brick walkway that led to the bayou, but today winter grays and browns still held sway.

"It is nice this afternoon. A welcome change from the cold weather we've been having."

She uncurled her legs from beneath her paisley skirt and rested her hands in her lap. "I'm a little ashamed of myself for frittering away the day like this. I should be at Maude's, or the shop, setting things to rights."

Luc studied her for a moment with shrewd blue eyes before he spoke again. "You've had a tough couple of days. Maude's things will wait. The Lagniappe Ladies took care of all the perishables in Maude's house. Her neighbor is feeding her cat. There's no reason for you to wear yourself out sorting through her things until you're rested and ready." He set the tea tray on a small wrought-iron table beside her left hand, seated himself in the chair on the other side of it, and began to pour the tea with none of the self-consciousness most men would exhibit performing such a feminine task. But then he was an innkeeper, and a hotelier by trade, she reminded herself, at ease with such rituals of hospitality.

He was certainly easy on the eyes, wearing a silky black polo shirt and a pair of stone-gray slacks with a knife-sharp crease.

"These muffins are wonderful," she said hurriedly when he caught her absentmindedly licking melted sugar from her fingers. She hoped he wasn't reading her thoughts. "What kind are they?" She looked down at the crumbs on her plate. She hadn't even known she was hungry, but she'd eaten a scone and two of the mini-muffins—and was thinking about trying a third.

He pointed them out. "Honey orange. Cranberry walnut and blueberry."

"They're marvelous. Just like the nut bread I had for breakfast."

"I'll pass the word on to the baker, Loretta Castille. She's starting her own business and she'll appreciate the compliment."

"I wish I could bake like this." She didn't even own baking dishes. She seldom cooked, seldom ate at home. Her business was entertaining the prospective philanthropic donors of her firms' clients at Houston's finer restaurants, not cooking for them herself.

"It's an art as well as a skill."

"I never looked at it like that, but you're right." With a smile she gave in to temptation and popped a bite-size blueberry muffin into her mouth. When she'd finished her second cup of tea she knew she couldn't put off her trip into Indigo any longer. "I think I can make it through to dinner now."

She stood up and Luc stood with her. "I noticed there's turtle soup on the menu tonight at the Blue Moon when I drove through town earlier," he said. "I highly recommend it."

"Thanks, I'll keep it in mind." He held the door for her while she went inside to get her purse.

"If you want some company, I'm not busy," Luc said easily, but his blue gaze was still assessing, and all too perceptive.

"Thanks, but no. I'll be fine." She appreciated his offer, but she realized she needed to do this on her own.

Still, she was almost sorry she'd turned him down when she opened the door to Maude's house and was greeted with the familiar smell of cats, old leather and lavender sachet that she'd always associated with her godmother. The room was small, packed with heavy, thirties-era upholstered furniture, except for a nearly new flat-screen TV that looked out of place on the drum table where it was sitting. The walls were papered in a faded rose print, covered in landscapes and amateurish still lifes, juxtaposed with fretwork shelves packed chockablock with all manner of glassware and china figurines.

It was all so familiar, and yet sadly empty without Maude's bustling presence. Sophie sat down on the edge of the sagging chintz sofa and covered her face with her hands, the tears she'd felt burning at the back of her eyelids all afternoon spilling over at last. "Goodbye, Nana," she whispered into the quiet. "I'll miss you, and so will Grandma Darlene."

She had spent so many happy times with Maude when she was younger. Sophie was an only child. Her parents were successful, driven people, her mother now a state district court judge, her father head of the prestigious fund-raising firm of Clarkson and Hillman. Her grandmother was a loving woman, but with a full and busy life of her own that left little time for playing dolls and dress-up with a sometimes lonely little girl.

But it hadn't been that way when she'd visited Maude in Indigo. There were always vintage clothes in the storage area of Past Perfect to play dress-up in, and bedraggled baby dolls to clean up and bedeck in the yellowing doll clothes that had belonged to Maude herself. She had had summer friends to go on bike rides with along the bayou, swimming in the pool the town had built in the river park, ice-cream cones and ice-cold watermelon slices at the church festivals that went on almost every weekend…and then the summer she turned eighteen…Alain.

She remembered him as he had been in those days, thin and gangly, his big hands dangling from skinny arms, his hair long and slightly shaggy, the way all the boys were wearing it then, his nose too big for his face. He didn't look like that anymore. He'd grown into his body and his nose. He was harder and stronger…and she wasn't going to think about him anymore.

Suiting action to thoughts, she stood up and walked down the hallway toward the kitchen, peeking into the room that was always hers when she stayed with Maude. Nothing had changed since her last visit, the familiar pale-yellow wallpaper festooned with purple honeysuckle, the colors faded a tiny bit more than they'd been in the spring, the muted blues and reds of the Oriental carpet, the same walnut armoire and dressing table, the same white candlewick spread on the squeaky iron bedstead and lace curtains at the window.

She went across the hall to stand in the doorway of Maude's bedroom. The bed, with its antique wedding-ring quilt, was neatly made, her chenille robe, the same one she'd been wearing as long as Sophie could remember, folded at the end of the bed, her slippers peeping out from beneath the coverlet. Her friends had taken care to make it look as if she'd just stepped out of the room, not left it forever.

The kitchen, spanning the width of the narrow house, as the living room did, was just as she remembered it, too. Chrome table and chairs, white-painted, glass-front cupboards and scrubbed pine counters and the collection of china hen-and-rooster salt and pepper shakers on the windowsill above the sink. Surely she didn't have to start dismantling the bits and pieces of Maude's life right this minute? Tomorrow or the next day would be soon enough. She left the house, locking the door softly behind her. She swallowed hard to dislodge the lump in her throat.

The house could wait until she was ready, but Past Perfect was a different matter. It was a viable business concern and she needed to make arrangements for someone to run it until it could be sold. She decided to leave her car where it was and walk the two blocks to the town square. The open grassy area was dotted with huge live oak trees and bisected by brick walkways. A statue of a confederate soldier stood at their intersection. On the statue's cracked marble base, the names of the Indigo boys who had died in the Civil War were inscribed. First on the list was Alexandre Valois, who had built the opera house and whose widow had paid for the monument. The were also a Robichaux, two Picards, Maude's great-grandfather and a cousin, and several Boudreauxs, members of Alain's family.

She smiled. It pleased her that she remembered at least a few of the bits and pieces of Indigo history that Maude had told her over the years. One or two people passed by and nodded pleasantly, trying politely not to stare too hard. Sophie nodded back, recognizing them from the wake and the funeral, but her attention remained focused on the opera house.

The building needed painting she realized as she drew closer, and Marjolaine and Hugh Prejean, the old gentleman she'd spoken to at the wake, were right, the roof did need work. She could see half a dozen places where the shingles were missing just from where she stood. The almost simultaneous blows of Hurricanes Katrina and Rita a couple of years earlier had damaged the old structure even more than the occupation of Union soldiers had.

Sophie turned the heavy key that had been among the items in Maude's purse in the lock and opened one of the big double doors. Once more the scents of lavender and old leather and dust tickled her nostrils, but this time her sorrow was mixed with happiness. She had always loved Past Perfect. The summer she had been so madly in love with Alain, she had imagined herself living in Indigo and working with her god-mother among all these mementos of a bygone day.

Of course, when she'd gotten home to Houston, her mother had disabused her of that notion pretty quickly. And even if she'd had the courage to stand up for herself, Alain's short, curt letter breaking off their secret engagement because he had decided to enter the army to earn money for college had put an end to her girlish fantasies.

At least until that other summer, the short window of time after her divorce when she'd thought they might find that lost love again, before Alain's pregnant wife had discovered them in each other's arms.

In this very building.

The bell above the door jingled a greeting as she stepped inside. Past Perfect's showroom occupied the lobby of the opera house, a space twice as long as it was deep. The counter, a relic of a demolished Memphis department store, stood directly in front of the tall, carved double doors that led into the auditorium.

That brought her up short for a moment, but she shook off the shiver of embarrassment and remorse. She didn't have to go into the storage area with its raised stage and two tiny bow-fronted boxes high on the wall—not yet, not unless she wanted to. Eventually she would—sometime when she wasn't thinking about Alain, but of what a treasure trove of make-believe the opera house had been for a young girl. The narrow stairs to the boxes had been steep and a little scary to climb, but when she was up there looking down, her imagination had had no trouble at all turning the creaky wooden folding chair on which she perched into a velvet and gilt one. She'd populated the shabby seats below with beautiful ladies in hoop skirts and dashing gentlemen in gray uniforms with plumed hats and swords at their sides, hearing voices and music in her head that had once brought the empty space to life. Those were the memories she'd keep in her thoughts when she did venture inside.

She wandered farther into the jumble of furniture and knickknacks, realizing as she always did that her godmother's seemingly haphazard arrangement of merchandise actually facilitated the flow of customer traffic, leading them eventually to the assortment of antebellum Indigo souvenirs, candles and personal care products, with their generous markups, that brought her a good deal of income from less-than-enthusiastic antiquers and tourists who might otherwise leave the premises without taking out their wallets and credit cards.

She wondered who among her Indigo acquaintances would be qualified to take over the operation of Past Perfect. Sadly, over the past seven years, those acquaintances had dwindled to a handful. But she was getting ahead of herself, thinking about reopening the store. First she needed to have an inventory taken for estate purposes, both here and at the house.

She might as well get an idea of what she was up against.

She headed resolutely for the tall, carved doors leading into the auditorium, took a breath and twisted the handles to throw them wide. The doorbell tinkled and Sophie swiveled her head. Beyond the wavy glass, a tall man in a dark shirt and a gray Stetson was silhouetted against the bright afternoon sun. Alain. Her past had come back to haunt her.

CHAPTER FIVE

"Afternoon, Sophie," he said as she used both hands to open the big front door. Maude Picard had been a no-nonsense, down-to-earth woman, but when it came to Past Perfect she'd given her inner belle free rein. Alain moved gingerly into the minefield of trailing scarves, little crystal bowls of sneeze-inducing potpourri and spindly-legged furniture that threatened to trip him up whenever he set foot inside the place.

Sophie didn't close the door right away and he caught her glancing surreptitiously out over the square. Damn it, was she still gun-shy about the time Casey Jo had caught them in the back room? Hell, they hadn't done anything wrong, but Casey Jo had jumped to her usual wrong-headed conclusion and come at them like some kind of fury.

He'd had every intention of filing for divorce before that day his wife had boomeranged back into his life six months pregnant, but he'd never gotten a chance to tell Sophie that. As a matter of fact, he'd never been alone with her since, that he could recall.

"Afternoon, Alain." *Ah-lane.* He liked the way she said his name, still giving it the lilting French pronunciation that had more to do with a high-class private school education than the time she'd spent in Indigo as a kid.

"Saw you walking across the square so I thought I'd drop by and ask if you needed help with anything." It wasn't much of an excuse but it was the only one he had.

She didn't let go of the door handle. "I'm just looking the place over." He saw her throat muscles work as she swallowed. "This is harder than I thought it would be...going through Maude's things. I thought maybe it would be easier starting with the shop rather than the house, but I was mistaken." She looked around and he caught the liquid sheen of unshed tears in her eyes. "It will have to be inventoried, won't it, for taxes and probate, that kind of thing?"

"I imagine it will. Were you her only heir?" Maybe if he kept the conversation solidly rooted in practicalities she'd stop looking like she was going to cry. Or worse yet, cut and run the first chance she got.

"I'm the executor, too. She made a lot of bequests. The library, the historical society, the church. I want to do my best to carry them out."

He knew Maude had left Sophie the house and its contents. The old woman had told his grandmother that much about her will and Yvonne had passed the tidbit of information along to him. "If you decide not to run the place yourself, you'll probably have to have an auction to get rid of all this stuff."

"I know." She relaxed enough to shut the door but she wrapped her arms around her waist, maybe to ward off the chill of the unheated room, more likely as an unspoken warning to him not to violate her personal space. "I haven't even gone into the storage area yet." Her tone of voice told him she had no intention of doing so while he was around. "I don't know if I'm allowed to reopen the shop until I talk to Nana's lawyer. And even then I'm not familiar with anyone in Indigo that I could hire to run the place."

"I could probably help you there. Maybe Hugh Prejean would fill in for a few weeks? He's mostly retired from the library now. He knows as much about antiques as anyone around. There are one or two others I could suggest."

"Thanks. I'll keep Mr. Prejean in mind." She waved her hand in a graceful feminine gesture that made his gut tighten a little as he remembered the softness of her fingers on his skin on a long-ago summer day. "I expect she'd want me to try and find a buyer for the business, not just sell off her assets. And then there are the terms of the lease for the opera house. I haven't a clue what they are."

He made himself stop thinking of what had once been and start concentrating on the here and now. "You don't have to settle everything today. Like you said, after you meet with Maude's lawyer will be soon enough to start making plans." He laid his hat on the glass-topped counter that held an array of costume jewelry and tucked his thumbs in his utility belt just to have something to do with them.

"I suppose so. The first decision I have to make is to rethink how long I'm going to stay in Indigo."

Alain felt his heart rate accelerate. "You have work waiting back in Houston?" What he wanted to ask wasn't whether she had work waiting, but if she had *someone* waiting.

"Nothing pressing at the moment. We just wrapped up a big fund-raising campaign for Northeastern College near Beaumont."

"Never heard of it," he said, figuring honesty was the best policy with her. "Must not have much of a football team." He tried a little self-deprecating humor and almost got a smile out of her.

"No, you probably haven't heard of it. It's a small church-affiliated liberal arts school. I spearheaded the campaign that brought in two million dollars in new endowments over the past eighteen months," she said proudly.

He didn't know much about fund-raising beyond the high-school kids selling magazine subscriptions and frozen pizzas to pay for their class trip, but for a small college with no winning football team, two mil in endowments seemed impressive. "Congratulations."

"I am kind of proud of it myself. Takes a lot of persuasion to come up with that kind of donations when they don't have any sports program to speak of." She smiled then, letting him know she'd gotten his joke, and it seemed to him when she did, the bright winter sunshine beyond the windows dimmed in comparison. She wandered over to a claw-foot drum table and picked up a china teacup painted with tiny pink and yellow roses. The pink of the flowers matched her nail polish.

"I never had the chance to tell Nana Maude about it."

Her hair was still a riot of curls but the color had darkened a little over the years from pale moonlight to sun-ripened wheat. She'd pushed the heavy mass behind her ears and held it back with a pair of tortoise-shell clips. His fingers itched to see if it was still as soft and silky as it had been a dozen or more years ago. From the looks of it, it was. "I was so caught up in the campaign that I missed coming to see her over the holidays. I…" Her voice wavered a moment, then steadied. "I thought my grandmother and I could come together for a long visit in a month or so. Now it's too late."

"Maude went quickly," he said. "Doc Landry told me there was almost no pain. She just sat down in her chair and went to sleep."

"I know." Her voice was very soft and he had to strain to hear. "He told me that, too, at Savoy's, when he stopped by to pay his respects. But it doesn't change the fact I didn't get to say goodbye."

He picked up his Stetson from the counter and twisted the brim in his hands. The powerful urge to comfort her took him by surprise. He'd thought of Sophie Clarkson a lot over the past five years since his divorce, but he'd never let it get out of control. Until Maude died. Since then she'd been on his mind almost constantly. Not a good sign.

He settled his hat on his head. He could handle it though. He wasn't eighteen anymore, so full of hor-mones and first love that he couldn't think straight. Or even twenty-eight for that matter, daring to hope for a few days that summer before Dana was born that he might be able to sort out his life and get a second chance with her.

What did they say? Third time's the charm?

Not for this country boy.

She was a damned desirable woman, but he'd sworn off women, desirable or otherwise, until his kids were raised and on their own. He wasn't being noble. He didn't have much choice with an unpredictable, unstable ex-wife like Casey Jo in the picture.

"I think I have customers," Sophie said, putting the teacup back on its saucer. She inclined her head toward the door, and sure enough, there were his kids, just off the school bus, Guy carrying his sister's shiny new Bratz book bag along with his own. At fifteen, his son was tall and awkward, all gangly arms and legs that he didn't seem to know what to do with when he wasn't on the football field or the basketball court. He reminded Alain of himself at that age.

Dana was small and slender with jet-black hair and emerald eyes, just turned seven and the spitting image of her mother. Except that even at seven, Casey Jo wouldn't have worn her hair stuffed up under a backwards baseball cap with a Saints sweatshirt and scuffed runners. Casey Jo was all girl, and at the moment, his daughter wanted to be anything but.

"I'll tell them to wait in the truck," he said, heading for the door, but Sophie beat him to it.

"No, let them come in. I'd like to meet them."

"Hi, Daddy." Dana bounced into the store and wrapped her arms around his arm, avoiding the holstered .45 Sig, billy club and mace container at his waist.

"Hello, *petite*," he said cradling her head with his free hand. "How was school today?" He spoke in Cajun French, but she answered in English, too shy to practice the French words in front of a stranger.

"Good. I was the first one done with my writing paper. I can do a whole paragraph."

"Bon."

She kept hold of his arm and peeked at Sophie from the corner of her eye. "Who's she?" Dana asked shyly. This time she spoke in French and Alain saw Sophie tighten her lips to keep from smiling.

"Dana, this is Sophie Clarkson. Miss Maude's goddaughter."

"Hello, Dana."

"Hi."

"And this is my son."

"Hello, Guy." The French pronunciation of the single syllable slid like warm butter over his skin. He wasn't the only one affected by Sophie's charm. She turned her stunning smile on his son and the boy's mouth dropped open and hung there for a moment or two before he pulled himself together and shook her proffered hand.

"Nice to meet you," he finally managed to get out.

"We did meet before, when you were a little boy," Sophie said.

Guy cocked his head, then shrugged. "I'm sorry I don't remember."

"It was a long time ago," she said softly, and Alain wondered if he only imagined a hint of regret in her words.

"What are you two doing here?" Alain asked to change the subject so his own memories of that second time around with Sophie wouldn't stir enough to keep him awake in the middle of the night.

"She saw the Explorer parked out front and insisted on coming inside," Guy explained, motioning to his little sister. "Grandma must have worked late today and wasn't there to pick us up at the bus stop. Good thing it wasn't raining or she'd have been soaked. She forgot her umbrella."

"I didn't forget it. I didn't take it with me. The sun was shining when I woke up. It's still shining." Dana swung on Alain's hand as she dismissed her brother's lecture. "He doesn't care if I get rained on. All he really wants is for you to buy him a car so he can drive it to school."

"I do, too, care," Guy insisted, but he turned slightly pink and looked down at his shoes.

Dana snorted. "Yeah, sure." She might be only seven but she had her big brother's number when it came to getting himself a set of wheels.

"Dad—"

"Knock it off, you two. Thanks for looking out for your sister's welfare, son. But you won't be sixteen for another three months. Time enough to talk about getting a car in the spring."

Guy opened his mouth, then thought better of what he was going to say and shoved his hands in his pockets. "I've got conditioning. Can you drop me off at home so I can get my gym bag?"

"I suppose." He'd been headed that direction for an end-of-shift patrol of the neighborhood, anyway.

"I'll wait in the truck." Guy hunched his shoulder and gave Sophie an apologetic smile. "It was nice meeting you, but I need to get out of here. I feel like I'm going to break something every time I move in this place."

Sophie laughed out loud. She couldn't help herself. He really did look afraid to move an inch from where he was standing. Suddenly she remembered how it felt to be not-quite-sixteen and suddenly at odds with your body. "I agree there are a lot of booby traps in this place. I should probably do some rearranging—make it easier for the customers to move around. What do you think?"

"I think it's a good idea." He cast a wary eye around the overcrowded space. "A real good idea."

"I'll consider it. If I can find some help."

Guy glanced at his father. "I help out at the B&B sometimes. Mr. Carter could vouch for me. And I...I know a couple of guys who are good at moving furniture. We work pretty cheap."

"I'll remember that." She held out her hand once more. "Goodbye, Guy. It was nice meeting you, too."

He shook her hand, gave his father a half wave, half salute and loped out the door. While Sophie and Guy were talking, Dana had let go of her father's hand and wandered farther into the store. "I don't feel like I'm going to break anything," she said, running her fingers over a ratty-looking fox stole draped over the back of cane-bottomed chair. "I like this place just the way it is."

"Guys are different than girls, I keep telling you that," Alain said. Amusement mingled with a hint of exasperation laced his words.

"Maybe." Dana shrugged. It was obvious to Sophie that she wasn't ready to admit the fact. "I like old things."

"I do, too," Sophie replied. The little girl studied her closely.

"You do?"

"But I don't know as much about them as Nana Maude did," Sophie confessed. She resisted the urge to move closer to Alain's—and Casey Jo's—daughter. It was probably better if she kept her distance from the child.

"She used to tell me stories about the opera house and how it was a hospital during the Civil War when I came here with *Mamère* Yvonne." The corners of Dana's mouth turned down and her eyes darkened to the color of the slow-moving bayou when it passed beneath a live oak tree. "*Mamère* is sad that Miss Maude died."

"They were very good friends. I miss her, too. She was my Nana." Sophie dropped to her knees on the dusty floor, forgetting, almost as quickly as she'd made it, her promise to herself to keep her distance from Alain's daughter.

Dana nodded solemnly. "*Nana* means godmother. I'm learning Cajun from my dad." She reached out and patted Sophie's hand as softly as she'd patted the ratty fox stole. "*Mamère* is sad but she said that Miss Maude has gone to Heaven to be with Jesus and the saints and martyrs and her mama and papa. She will be happy there."

"That's true. Thank you for reminding me. I'll try and remember that when I'm missing her."

"Good. Can I go look at the stuffed animals?"

Sophie stood up, gazing around in genuine puzzlement. "Stuffed animals? I have no idea where they might be."

"Over here." Dana slipped along a corridor of glass cases, heading for a huge mahogany armoire in a shadowy back corner of the room. Distracted, she stopped midway down the aisle to study an item in one of the cases. "Your fiddle's still here, Daddy."

Sophie raised her eyes to Alain's bemused gaze. "Your fiddle? I didn't know you played the fiddle. I remember you played the bass guitar…years ago in a garage band." She remembered a lot more than that about the teenage Alain, but she wasn't going to reveal any of it. Especially her girlish dreams of being the mother of his children; a boy like Guy, a daughter like Dana, dreams that in that long-ago bayou summer hadn't seemed like fantasies at all, but only glimpses of the future she was sure would be hers. But her dreams hadn't come to pass, and Alain's children were his with Casey Jo. It had all happened a long time ago, but when the past was so close, as it was today, it still hurt. She followed Dana down the narrow aisle, not looking back at Alain for fear he might read her betraying memories in the expression on her face, or the look in her eyes.

"I didn't play the fiddle then. I took it up after my grandfather died. He left me his instrument. He was quite a musician in his day."

She lifted an eyebrow. "Since when do heavy metal bands like the Rotting Alligators—that was the name, wasn't it?—use a fiddle player?"

"God, you remember that? I was hoping no one did. I don't play in a heavy metal band anymore. Or in any band, but I have been studying Cajun fiddling. Took it up for *Mamère's* sake, to keep the family tradition alive, then I kind of got hooked. Don't have much time to play any more, but I try to keep my hand in."

"I don't understand how your fiddle got in Maude's display case." Sophie stopped beside Dana and studied the instrument in the case. Its neck was resting on a velvet cushion and even she, who was far from an expert, could tell it was handmade and probably quite valuable.

"It's not my fiddle. Wish it was, though. That was Maude's little joke, calling it mine. It's a Delacroix. He was a Cajun fiddle maker from over in St. Germain Parish. He was self-taught but a real artist." He traced the lines of the small violin through the glass. "See here, the inlay work along the bridge? It's magnolia and black gum. He always worked in native woods. The body's walnut—you can tell by the grain. He died a few years ago. Most of his instruments are in collectors' hands. This is one of the few that isn't. It's worth a pretty penny. Don't know why Maude didn't sell it long before now."

"Maybe she did want you to have it?" Sophie lifted her eyes to find him watching her, not the fiddle.

He grinned, and her heart gave a quirky little jump that made her catch her breath. "If she did, she never offered me a break on the price."

"I'd be willing to entertain your best offer." Sophie realized how provocative the words sounded as soon as they left her mouth.

The sun lines around his eyes tightened and the corners of his mouth hardened momentarily. His tone was as friendly as it had been a moment before, but still she felt the sting of his words. "It's out of my price range. Besides, I've got my granddaddy's fiddle and it's a good one. But thanks, anyway."

"Daddy, the stuffed animals are gone." Once more Dana had slipped away unnoticed and was standing in front of a heavy mahogany bookcase that was loaded with bric-a-brac, except for the top shelf, which was conspicuously empty. Dana was staring up at it with her head thrown back and her hands on her hips. Her tone was thoroughly disgusted. "They were here the last time *Mamère* Yvonne brought me here. Miss Maude gave me one of them. A green dragon. He's in my room. And Miss Maude said she'd give me another one when we came back. Do you know where they are, Miss Sophie?"

"I'm sorry, I don't. But I haven't had a chance to look in the storeroom yet."

"We can look now. I'll help you."

"I'm afraid I have other plans for the rest of the afternoon." Suddenly she wanted to be alone, away from Alain and the bittersweet memories his presence brought. Away from his little girl, who was so appealing, and who reminded her of all that was missing in her own life.

"Daddy, tell her we'll help her."

"You heard Miss Sophie. She has other plans. And you need to be getting home. Grandma Cecily will be wondering what happened to you."

"All right." If Dana's lower lip jutted out another millimeter, she'd be in a full-fledged pout. "I'll come back tomorrow or the next day," she said grudgingly after one last glance at the empty shelf.

"I'm sure I'll have located the stuffed animals by then."

"Goodbye," she said, still reluctant to leave. Her father gave her a gentle push toward the door.

"Goodbye, Dana. I'm so glad I got to meet you and your brother." Sophie had herself back in hand. Her smile and her words were genuine.

She was rewarded with a brilliant smile in return. "Me, too." Dana danced toward the front door, heedless of the china and glass on all sides, truly as at home in the crowded space as she'd claimed to be.

"She's charming, Alain," Sophie said truthfully. She'd managed to relegate the old hurts to a shadowy corner of her mind. "And Guy's a fine young man. I'll be glad to have him help me—" she lifted her hands in a gesture of indecision "—do what has to be done here."

"You don't have to give him work."

"I want to." That, too, was the truth. She could meet his eyes without flinching when she said it.

He watched her steadily for a moment, then nodded. "He'll do a good job."

"I'm sure he will. He's your son, after all." They both watched through the wavy glass of the many-paned windows as Dana hopped into the SUV through the door her brother held open for her.

Sophie studied Alain's face for a moment. His were the features of a man who had known hardship but who had never given in to it. A man who had fulfilled the potential she had sensed in the boy. "They're both great kids," he said quietly as he turned to leave. "They're my whole world, Sophie. That's why I stayed with their mother as long as I did."

"SOPHIE CLARKSON was in Past Perfect today," Cecily told her mother. She was holed up in her bathroom, sitting on the toilet lid with the portable phone from her bedroom, water running in the sink, whispering so Alain wouldn't overhear if he walked down the hall.

"What? I can't hear you, Cecily. You'll have to speak louder."

Cecily sighed and gave up. She switched to French. Alain's Cajun was pretty good but he wasn't as fluent as she and Yvonne. Most of the time she regretted so few of the family spoke the old tongue anymore, but tonight she was glad. "I said Sophie Clarkson was in Past Perfect today. She's evidently starting to look through the inventory. Dana was there and spoke to her."

"What was the little one doing at Maude's shop?"

"She and Guy were walking home from the school bus and saw Alain there and went inside," Cecily explained impatiently. She had her own thoughts, and misgivings, about her son spending time with Sophie Clarkson, but she didn't have time to indulge them right now. It was the shipment that was important. "We have to decide how to get the animals out of there before she notices them."

"I still can't hear you. Is that water running?"

Cecily shut off the faucet. "Sorry. My mind wandered there for a moment."

"Well, wander it back to the problem at hand. We've got to get inside Past Perfect and get our medicines."

Cecily sighed. "Yes, Mama, I know that."

"Grandma? Are you in there? I need to use the bathroom." Dana's voice came through the door, giving Cecily such a start she almost dropped the phone.

"I'll be out in a minute, honey. I'm just washing my hands." She turned the water back on.

"I've got to go, Mama. Dana needs the bathroom. I'll think of some way to get into Past Perfect."

"And how are you going to do that if you don't know how to turn off the alarm?"

"*Merde.*"

"Cecily!"

"Pardon, Mama. I didn't know Maude had installed an alarm for the place."

"The owner, or at least the lawyer, insisted on one. But Maude was always forgetting to set it. Most days she didn't remember to turn the deadbolt. Maybe Sophie doesn't know about it and it's still turned off. We'll have to find out before we break in."

"Grandma! I have to go. Now."

Cecily's head hurt. Her feet hurt. She'd put in a ten-hour day at the hospital and still had laundry to do. Instead of sitting in her recliner with Dana on her lap, reading a story, she was planning a B&E over the telephone with her seventy-five-year-old mother. It was bizarre.

"Are you still there?"

"Yes, Mama."

"You'll think of something. In the meantime I'll call Estelle and Willis and tell them not to worry, we'll get Willis's medicine for him by the end of the week." Yvonne broke the connection from her end.

Cecily stood up. The end of the week, eh? It was her weekend off. At least she wouldn't have to use up vacation days if she ended up in Alain's jail.

CHAPTER SIX

"HEY, WHAT ARE you doing still awake?" Alain opened the bedroom door so that light from the hallway crept over the hardwood floor to the edge of Dana's bed.

"I'm not sleepy," came the reply from the mound of pillows showing snowy white in the shadows. Dana claimed to hate anything girly, but her room was definitely feminine: pink-flowered wallpaper with sheer ruffled curtains at the window—like a garden, she insisted when he teased her about it, not like a *girl*. Alain sat down on the side of the bed and Dana, her eyes shining in the reflected light, scooted over so that her leg rested against his thigh.

"Why don't you try closing your eyes and thinking sleepy thoughts. That always helps."

"Not tonight." She was twisting the edge of her sheet between her fingers. When she was little she'd carried a fraying piece of her favorite baby blanket with her everywhere until it had literally fallen apart in her hands. She'd outgrown the need for a security blanket, but when she was tired, or upset, he would catch her twisting a lock of her hair, or worrying a bit of fabric the way she was now. "When I close my eyes I think of Momma."

Alain blew air through his nose. "What did Momma have to say when she called?" His mother had told him Casey Jo had phoned just before he got home from work and Dana had answered the phone before Cecily could get to it. He should have known his ex would try an end run around him to get to the kids. He'd attempted to get hold of her the last three nights to tell her there was no way he was going to allow the Disney World jaunt when it meant taking them out of school even for a couple of days, but she'd avoided his calls with more success than he and Cecily had avoided hers.

"She wants to come and get me to go to Disney World." Dana's eyes lit up at the mention of the theme park. "I…I told her I have to ask you first."

Alain ground his teeth and tried not to let his anger at Casey Jo show on his face or in his voice. "I know you'd really like to go."

"I would." She frowned. "But Guy doesn't want to. He told Momma he couldn't go because he has driver's ed classes. I can't believe he doesn't want to go to the Magic Kingdom. Can you?"

"He wants to get his driver's license really bad. Enough to give up a trip to Disney World it seems."

"Well, not me," Dana said with a great deal of certainty. "Momma says I can have breakfast with Cinderella and Snow White in the castle. Why doesn't Guy want to do that?" Her green eyes shone with anticipation and he couldn't suppress a smile. She looked so much like Casey Jo when she was excited about something that it made his throat ache. It hadn't been all bad times between them, and when he saw Dana like this, he remembered the good stuff, at least for a little while. "Can I go, Daddy, please?"

He hated always being the bad guy, but that's what happened when you had children with a woman who never wanted to grow up. While she ran off to follow her own selfish dreams, he got stuck with all the tough jobs. "We'll see," he said, not able to dash all her hopes. "But—"

"I know," she said, sounding suddenly much older than her seven years. "But Momma might change her mind."

"Yes, she might." He got himself back in hand and played the heavy. "And I don't like the idea of you missing school. You only have a two-day vacation. It's a long way to Florida."

"Maybe we can go when school's out," she said hopefully, but without much conviction. Even at seven she'd learned not to count on anything her mother planned.

She was tired and he didn't want a bout of tears at bedtime. "We'll talk about it some more after I get a chance to discuss it with your mom, okay?" He leaned over and gave her a kiss on the cheek. She locked her arms around his neck and kissed him back.

"Okay. I love you, Daddy," she whispered in French, then turned over on her side and curled into a ball under the covers.

"I love you, too, *petite*." He amended his earlier bitter reflection as he inhaled the scent of strawberry shampoo and warm, sweet, little-girl skin. You might get all the tough jobs being a single parent, but you also get all the hugs and baby kisses and I love yous, too. He stood up and walked to the window, looking out over the village he'd called home for nearly all his life. The place he'd chosen to raise his children.

Indigo was a pretty little town, not much crime, not much of a tax base, either. But enough to keep up the infrastructure and lure a few yuppies, tired of city life, to buy, build and rehab the old shotgun houses around the town square, and even a couple of the big Victorian white elephants on either side of his mother's twenties-era, Craftsman-style two-story. Still, he'd be lying if he said it was the center of the universe. That is, anyone else's universe other than his own.

He liked being Chief of Police. He liked looking after his neighbors and friends, their parents and grand-parents, kith and kin. He liked being able to drive his kids to school and pick them up at night, even if he did never really go off duty. More often than not he'd have to head out for traffic accidents and domestic disputes at all hours of the day and night. That was a cop's job, after all, and he was a cop, through to his bones. Had been ever since the army had made him an MP and he'd found his calling in life.

It hadn't always been that way. Once, a long time ago, he'd had other dreams—getting out of Indigo, heading to the big city, making a name for himself as a bass guitarist in Memphis or even L.A. But such grandiose plans hadn't lasted long after his dad died.

He'd grown up fast that summer he was nineteen, figured out that he wasn't going anywhere as long as his mom and two younger sisters needed him. But he'd been wrong there, too. Cecily was as determined as he was that he make something of himself. What they differed on was what that something would be. Alain smiled and turned from the window to gaze at his daughter once more.

Dana was sound asleep. He tucked the covers under her chin and tiptoed out of the room, shutting the door behind him. He went next door to his own room, smaller but with a view out over the backyard where he could glimpse the bayou on clear days. He hadn't been the greatest student in the world. Hell, you didn't have to be when you were going to take the music world by storm, so there weren't any scholarships for him the summer he graduated from high school. But Cecily was determined he go to college. No scholarships and no money. But there was the army, so he'd signed up for a four-year hitch and the college tuition bonus that came with it.

And then one June morning, Sophie Clarkson had strolled into the garage where he was working for his uncle Max until he was called up, and lit up his world. She had been willowy, blond and beautiful, perfect in every way. Rich and sophisticated, or so it seemed to him, and she took his breath away. He'd fallen in love on the spot. And wonder of wonders, she'd seemed to feel the same way.

He grabbed a basket of dirty clothes from the foot of his bed and snorted in self-derision as he headed down the stairs to the laundry room. "Face it, Boudreaux. She still does take your breath away."

"Did you say something, Alain?" his mother asked from the kitchen as he passed by.

"Nope," he lied. God, he was talking out loud to himself. That was a bad sign.

"Is Dana asleep?"

"Out like a light."

"Good. I was afraid she'd be too wound up to sleep after talking to her mother." Cecily hadn't taken the time to change from the set of maroon scrubs she'd worn to work that morning and she looked tired as she rested her elbows on the scarred top of the pine table that had sat in the middle of the kitchen floor for as long as Alain could remember. Familiar guilt jabbed at his gut. He was taking advantage of her, living here like this. It was time they moved out on their own.

He stood there holding the basket of dirty laundry, seeing his childhood home, his present sanctuary, in a different light. He knew the rent he paid for living here went a long way toward the upkeep on the old house. It was a monster to heat and cool. But his mother, and her mother before her, had grown up here. If he and the kids moved out, could she keep it? Did she even want to? The question surprised him a little. He hadn't thought of that before, his mom maybe wanting to move into a nice apartment in New Iberia or even Lafayette. Her life, her roots were planted so deep in the bayou soil he'd never pictured her any place else. But maybe it was time he did.

"Mom—"

She interrupted his attempt to broach the subject. "Are you planning to let Casey Jo take Dana to Florida?"

"Not if I can help it." He set the basket on the floor

and turned one of the high-backed pine chairs around backward to straddle the seat. "Even if she can afford the trip, I don't want her getting the idea she can take Dana out of school anytime the notion strikes her." He wasn't comfortable about letting his ex have the kids unsupervised. He never knew when one of her infrequent bouts of maternal feelings would kick in and she'd decide to try and keep them with her. Not that it would last long, just long enough to disrupt all their lives and cost him six months' salary for lawyer fees to get them back, but he wasn't going to take the chance if he could help it.

Cecily tucked a strand of graying hair into the braided knot on top of her head. "Good. Sometimes you're too soft-hearted." She got up and went to the coffeepot on the counter and poured a cup. His mom had a cast-iron stomach from drinking hospital coffee for thirty years. He'd be up all night if he drank coffee this late in the day. "If she's got the money to take the kids to Disney World, then she can damn well hand it over for their college funds, and I would have told her just that if I'd gotten to the phone before Dana did. Between you and me, I don't like it when she takes them out of the state. No telling what kind of idea that girl'll go and get in her head."

"Yeah, Mom. I thought of that, too." He stood up and heaved the laundry basket onto one hip. "Better get this load washed or it won't dry before bedtime."

"I'll get that," Cecily said, leaning back against the counter as she cradled her coffee mug in both hands. "You must have better things to do than laundry."

"You do, too," he said, heading for the washer and dryer on the back porch off the kitchen.

She snorted. "I don't know what it would be."

"Same here," he laughed. "We're both just homebodies."

"You're too young to be thinking that way."

"Hey, I'm just glad I've got a full duty roster for the weekend. I might even get the magnolia in the backyard trimmed for you. It's your weekend off. Why don't you do something special for yourself? Go out to dinner. See a movie. Shop."

She gave him a quick, almost guilty glance over the top of her mug. "Uh…no. I…I think I'll just work around the house. Unless…" She turned away and poured the rest of her coffee into the sink, her voice strained. "Unless your grandmother has something planned for me to do."

SHE WAS GONE when Alain returned from loading the washer. Guy had his head inside the refrigerator. He and Dana could stand that way for hours if he let them. Alain wondered if it was too late to bring *Mamère* Yvonne over for a couple of days, establish her at the kitchen table, and let her browbeat them into a healthy state of reluctance about wasting electricity, as she'd done for him and his sisters. He still couldn't stand in front of an open fridge for more than thirty seconds without feeling guilty about it. "Nothing in there's going to mutate into anything else while you're watching," he said, coming to stand beside his son.

"I'm starving," the teen muttered.

"We ate less than two hours ago."

"I'm a growing boy. I don't suppose I could take the truck and run out to the Gator Hole for a pizza?" The Gator Hole was an old roadhouse, just outside the town limits, that had been converted into a pizza place and carryout a dozen or so years ago. It was a hangout for the local kids. The owner, Eddie Larouche, had been a classmate of Alain's in high school. He kept the kids under control and in return Alain and his small force kept an eye on the place even though it was technically outside his jurisdiction.

"You suppose right."

"There's nothing to eat in here."

"There's got to be something. I bought a hundred and fifty dollars' worth of groceries two days ago."

"Toilet paper and dishwashing soap. I can't eat those."

Alain wasn't going to be suckered into an argument he couldn't win. He grabbed a can of soda and a package of cheddar cheese and shoved them in his son's hands. "Make do. There's a box of those onion crackers you like in the pantry."

"No more onion crackers. Gives me bad breath." Guy made a face at the offering, but headed for the tall narrow pantry beside the stove. Bad breath? Was it a girl that had brought on this sudden consideration for others? "Did you know Mom called tonight?" the boy asked as he pulled a paring knife out of the drawer beside the stove. "She still wants to take us to Disney World."

"I know, Dana told me." Alain grabbed a bottle of water off the shelf and shut the refrigerator door.

"I told her forget it." Guy dropped into a chair and propped both feet on another one, slouching down on his spine. His voice had changed over the winter. He didn't sound like a boy now, but an angry young man. "I told her she could wire the money she's planning to spend on me into my college account. Like that's ever gonna happen," he finished with a sneer.

"You'd better not have used that tone of voice," Alain said automatically.

"What does it matter?" The tone was still defiant but he didn't quite meet Alain's eye. "I hardly ever talk to her anyway."

"She's your mother. You should show that much respect."

Guy snorted and shoved the point of the paring knife into the block of cheese. "Respect, that's a hoot."

"All right." Alain held up his hand in a gesture of surrender. It was an old argument between them, one that wasn't going to be solved tonight. Guy had been five the first time his mother took off to "find herself," ten when she'd left for good. In between those years she'd confused and disappointed him often enough that he'd given up waiting for her to come back. They barely spoke. Casey Jo kept trying, and crying on Alain's shoulder when she got the chance, but it was her own fault, and until she grew up and faced that fact, Alain didn't hold out much hope for her relationship with their son. "Then I expect you to at least be polite."

Guy snorted again. There was hurt and confusion beneath his anger, though he tried hard to hide it. "I was polite. But I'm not going to Disney World with her and you better not let Dana go, either," he finished darkly.

"I don't intend to."

"No matter how much Grandma Marie cries about it, right?"

Alain met his son's eyes, so like his own at that age, and saw the worries of a man reflected in their navy-blue depths. "I'll stand my ground."

"Good. 'Cause once Dana thinks about it and Mom starts sending her all those little brochures and stuff you get from the travel agent, she'll make our lives miserable trying to get you to change your mind. Then something will happen and she won't get to go. I don't want Dana getting her heart broken."

"Is that the only thing you're worried about?"

Guy hacked off a piece of cheese. "She's always trying to get Dana to come live with her. Paints a real good picture of what it would be like. She used to try the same line of bull with me."

"Yeah, I know that, too." No use saying Casey Jo loved him and Dana…in her way. It was a lame explanation and they both knew it. Alain looked down at his half-empty bottle of water and wished it was a beer. He'd known tonight was only the opening skirmish of the Tinker Bell Wars. There would be more battles to come. And, as usual, even if he won, he would lose, too. He would come off looking like the heavy and Casey Jo would play the injured party and Dana and Guy would be caught in the middle.

Guy stomped out of the kitchen to finish his homework and Alain headed for the back porch. The washing machine had just entered the spin cycle, and rather than go back to the kitchen to wait it out, he propped his shoulder against the screen door and stared up into the night sky. The breeze off the bayou carried a chill but with the underlying promise of spring. Winters were cold and damp in this part of Louisiana but they were short, and in a few weeks people would be starting to work in their gardens, and by the end of March, warm weather would be back.

Would Sophie Clarkson still be in Indigo come spring? He doubted it. Maude's estate wasn't large. Once she got the paperwork out of the way and found someone to run Past Perfect, or an auction house to appraise the inventory and sell it off for her, she'd head back to Houston. Never to return.

Was he going to let that happen? He hadn't been in love with her for a long time, but there was still something there, a longing, a yearning deep inside him that had never gone away, even when he'd denied its existence all the years of his marriage to Casey Jo

Except for that one short week the summer before Dana was born, when it had almost chipped its way out of the locked vault of his heart and come to life again.

He stared at the stars visible through the bare branches of the magnolia tree his grandfather had planted beside the back step sixty years ago. The moon had risen over the bayou and shadows danced along the ground as the big tree's branches swayed in the night breeze. He shivered as the cold air penetrated his shirt.

He'd never made love to Sophie in the wintertime. Never slept with her beneath a warm blanket while cold

winter rains pounded the window beside the bed. He
wanted that, he realized with a sudden fierce longing.
He wanted to make slow love to her in the dark of a long
winter's night. Their teenage lovemaking had been as
heated as the Louisiana sun on their skin, as incendi-
ary as lightning bolts in a summer storm. He'd figured
they had their whole lives ahead of them to make love.
But their love hadn't lasted forever. It hadn't lasted
through a single change of seasons.

Her parents had come for her in early September,
looking much the same as they had at Maude's funeral,
tanned, toned and successful. To their credit, Donner
and Jessica Clarkson hadn't forbidden her to see him
again. They'd only asked her to wait until Christmas,
when he'd returned from basic training, to accept his
ring. And then they'd whisked her back to Houston, to
the life she'd always known.

Outside of rare phone calls, their only connection
had been her perfumed little notes on monogrammed
stationery chronicling the parties she'd attended, the
lunches with friends, shopping trips with her mother,
sorority rushes and college mixers that were as alien to
his world as life as an army grunt's wife would be to
hers. It hadn't taken him long to come to his senses. The
invasion of Kuwait had just taken place. Already there
were rumors of war. He knew he might get sent
overseas. He knew he might even get killed. So he had
broken off their almost-engagement. Noble, self-sacri-
ficing. Stupid as hell.

She'd called and she'd cried and declared she would
love him forever, but he'd stood firm and eventually she

gave up trying. Her last little perfumed note to him had been polite and reserved. She had wished him the best of luck in his life, and hoped he did the same for her.

Looking back from where he stood now, Alain figured letting her go had been the biggest mistake he'd ever made.

CHAPTER SEVEN

IT WAS RAINING again. Sophie pulled her car into the space beside the opera house where Maude had always parked, and made a dash for the porch. In the ten days since her godmother's funeral it had rained more often than the sun had shone. But at least today the rain was coming straight down, not being blown around by a chill breeze.

Still, she was thankful for the heavy black cardigan she wore over her cowl-necked, raspberry shell and black jeans. It was February now and not as cold as it had been in late January, but it was still a long way from warm. A long way from the steamy, almost tropical heat of a bayou summer.

Sophie made a face at her wavy reflection in the glass of the opera-house doors. There she went again, letting her mind slip too close to the past. She had thought her overnight trip to Houston to gather more suitable clothes and fill her parents in on her plans to stay in Indigo for a few weeks longer would have helped clear her mind of thoughts of Alain Boudreaux and what might have been, but just the opposite had occurred. She thought of him all the time—memories of him as a boy that enchanted summer, and even more disturbingly, fantasies of him as the man he now was.

She shook the raindrops from the slouchy black hat she'd shoved on her head in a vain attempt to keep the mass of curls under control, and inserted the heavy key into the old-fashioned deadbolt that secured the opera-house door. She didn't even glance at the keypad of the security system that had been affixed to the wide door frame. It wasn't turned on and she hadn't been able to find the instructions on how to reset it or even a contact number for the company that had installed it. She supposed Alain might have the combination on record at the jailhouse, but she hadn't asked him for it and hoped she didn't have to.

It didn't surprise her that she couldn't find the code. Maude's filing system, both personal and business, was as eccentric as she had been. It would take weeks to sort everything out. But Sophie was going to start working at it in earnest today, and if she didn't find what she was looking for, she'd give up and call Alain. Maude may have felt the contents of Past Perfect were safe without the electronic warning system, but she wasn't so sure.

She'd talked to her grandmother when she was in Houston, a breathtakingly expensive overseas call to New Zealand, where she and Sophie's grandfather were making a pilgrimage to the *Lord of the Rings* movie sites as part of her birthday tour. Darlene had promised to come to Indigo after her return to the States and help Sophie go through Maude's personal effects.

"Go back to La Petite Maison," Darlene had said in her eminently practical way. "Be comfortable. The house can wait." But the business really needed to be up and running again, or turned over to a reputable appraiser and auctioneer so that the inventory could be liquidated before the enervating heat of a southern Louisiana summer set in and made the buyers too hot and cranky to pay top dollar for the merchandise.

Sophie smiled again as she recalled her grandmother's words. The advice to ignore the house was blunt, but exactly what Maude's lawyer had told her. If she was going to put the inventory of Past Perfect on the block by spring, she had to start now.

As soon as she walked through the door, the familiar smell of old roses and lavender, dust and times-gone-by rose to greet her. She felt strangely as if she'd come home, and was a little bit reluctant to part with all of this. She wasn't going to go there, either. She was a fund-raiser and a good one, not an antique dealer in a small bayou town.

She shut the door behind her, sailed the slouchy hat onto the counter as she passed and opened the big double doors that led to the auditorium of the opera house one at a time, hooking them against the walls with claw-shaped iron hooks that had probably been forged by one of the slaves on the Valois plantation a hundred and fifty years ago.

She turned around and just stared. The daylight coming from the high four-over-four windows was gray and diffused, but there was more than enough to see what confronted her. The space before her was filled with boxes of books, camelback horsehair sofas and turn-of-the-last-century dining suites, the tables stacked high with sets of Depression-era china and boldly colored Fiesta ware. An eighteenth-century fainting couch was covered with hats and handbags that ranged from Jackie Kennedy pillboxes to Victorian garden hats bedecked with faded silk flowers and frayed ribbons. More boxes still unopened, and smaller tables, their surfaces hidden by dozens and dozens of china vases and figurines, filled the wide aisle that bisected the rows of dusty velvet-seated chairs that fronted the stage.

She turned her head, finding bed frames stacked against the wall and a dozen glass and china hurricane lamps marching up one of the narrow stairways to the private boxes that had been her magical childhood hideaway. On her right was a pair of five-drawer metal filing cabinets, their tops piled with baby boomer-era board games in worn cardboard boxes, and a set of green Depression-glass cups and saucers.

Sophie sat down with a thump on a cane-bottomed chair that protested her weight with an ominous squeak. She could never remember Maude carrying so much inventory. "This will take forever," she said out loud.

The bell above the front door jingled and a female voice called out a greeting in French. She recognized the voice; it belonged to Alain's mother, Cecily. For a moment Sophie was tempted to stay where she was, mostly hidden from the sales floor by the big open doors, but then another voice spoke and she was on her feet.

"Hello, Mrs. Boudreaux. Hello, Dana." Alain's daughter was wearing a red Winnie the Pooh raincoat and matching hat over jeans and a lightweight turtleneck sweater. Her smile showed a gap where she'd lost a tooth since Sophie had last seen her.

"Hello, Sophie," Cecily said, leaning her umbrella against the wall before following her granddaughter into the storage area. "We just thought we'd stop by and see how you were getting along."

"I'm trying to get a handle on all this." Sophie spread her hands to encompass the antiques crowding around them on three sides. "I'm going to need more than just Guy's help to deal with this stuff. I'll probably need the entire high-school basketball team. I had no idea Nana Maude had this much inventory."

"She had several pickers working for her. There've been a lot of sales around here over the last year or so. Lots of people gave up and moved after Hurricane Katrina and Rita hit. Maude paid top dollar and people were eager to sell to her, even if some of their things weren't as valuable as they'd hoped."

"Yes, of course. I didn't think of that."

Cecily shrugged. "Hurricanes are part of life down here. Always have been, always will be, I suppose."

"I understand this building sustained some damage from those storms, too."

"Put a big hole in the roof. Insurance paid to have it patched, but they wouldn't shell out for an entire new roof. That's what it really needs."

Automatically the two women looked up as though the ceiling had become transparent, then realized what they had done and began to laugh. Sophie relaxed slightly. She didn't know Alain's mother well, had only met her in passing over the years. There had been no reason for them to spend time together once she and Alain broke up. She regretted that. Cecily Boudreaux was an intelligent, no-nonsense woman who'd had her share of hard times, but still managed to enjoy life. Sophie would like to know her better. Perhaps today was a chance to start doing just that.

Dana began to tug on her grandmother's hand. "Grandma, look. There's the box of animals. See, right over there on that bench."

Sophie followed Dana's pointing finger with her eyes. On the seat of the high-backed, mirrored coat rack, half-hidden behind a raccoon coat that had been the height of fashion on VJ Day, was a shallow plastic storage box filled with colorful stuffed toys. "Are those the animals you were talking about the other day?" Sophie asked, picking her way around a particularly ugly chair made of animal horns. "The ones Nana Maude puts out on display in the armoire?"

Dana was jumping up and down. "Yes. Yes."

"Okay, let's see what we have here." Sophie picked up the container and set it on a slightly wobbly table. She poked a finger into the nest of stuffed toys. There was a frog and a teddy bear, a monkey and a small horse among others. Some were quite professional-looking, others more amateurish. She picked up the teddy and blinked in surprise at the amount affixed to the small white tag stapled into his paw. "Four hundred and seventy-five dollars? And this frog has an eighty-dollar tag." It was a cute teddy, well made, but certainly not worth that amount, and the frog...well, one of its legs was almost an inch shorter than the other, giving it a decidedly lopsided appearance. She glanced at Alain's mother and saw her face had lost its color.

"There's been a mistake in the labeling, I imagine," Cecily said, her voice just a shade too bright and a little loud. "My mother's cousin makes them for Maude... I mean she made, them for Maude."

Sophie glanced at the mailing label on the storage container. "Your mother's cousin lives in Nova Scotia?"

"Yes. She...she loves to sew, and Maude has a small group of customers that are sort of collecting her work...like Beanie Babies. You remember how popular they were?" She cleared her throat.

"But four hundred and seventy-five dollars?"

Dana was busy pawing through the box of animals. "Here's a cute kitty. Can I have this one someday?"

"Aren't they all spoken for?" Sophie asked.

"They usually are," Cecily told her, "but once in a while there's...one or two...that need a home. Maude puts those them out on the shelf. Usually she keeps them back here until their owners come for them. I...I'll pass the word around that the shipment arrived."

"Thank you. There doesn't seem to be any kind of inventory sheet."

"I'm sure it's here somewhere. Like I said, I'll pass the word around. Dana, come here." Cecily's voice was sharp. "We have to be going. You have homework." She walked past Sophie with a murmured apology, took the kitten the child was holding and put it back in the plastic tub. Her hands were shaking, Sophie noticed.

"Sophie, are you here?" She recognized Marjolaine Savoy's voice just as Cecily stumbled against the table holding the stuffed animals. A china shepherdess wobbled and a pair of wooden salt-and-pepper shakers shaped like outhouses bounced onto the faded carpet rolled up beneath the table. The whole container of little animals landed on the floor.

"I'm so sorry," Cecily mumbled. "I'll pick them up."

"Don't bother," Sophie began as Marjo called her name again.

"No. No. It was my fault. I'll get them back where they belong. Dana will help." Alain's daughter had already dropped onto her knees and started gathering the toys into her arms.

"All right," Sophie said and excused herself to Cecily with a smile as she stepped back into the shop. "Here I am, Marjo."

The funeral director held a large manila envelope in her hand. "The copies of Maude's death certificate came. When I saw your car outside I thought I'd drop them off here rather than make a trip out to the B&B."

"Thanks, Marjo. I'll need them when I go to the bank and the lawyer's office tomorrow." Sophie took the envelope and laid it on the counter, not really ready to look at the documents that detailed her godmother's death, but knowing she would have to sooner or later.

"If there's anything else I can help you with, just give me a ring." She peered over Sophie's shoulder into the auditorium. "How's the patch on the roof holding up? There's been a lot of rain the last couple of weeks."

"As far as I can tell everything's okay. I really haven't spent too much time back here."

Marjolaine peeked into the auditorium. "Oh. Hello, Cecily. Dana."

"Hello, Marjo," Cecily said, clutching the strap of her shoulder bag with one hand and Dana with the other. "We're just leaving. We stopped in to see if Sophie needed anything but she seems to be doing just fine."

"We picked up all the little animals," Dana piped up.

"Thank you, Dana. Come back soon," Sophie said. "And please tell Guy I'll be in touch about helping out around here." She would need expert advice on the value of the shop's inventory, but she could at least put the contents in some kind of order on her own.

"I'll do that. *Adieu*." Cecily hurried toward the door so quickly that Sophie had to remind her not to forget her umbrella.

Sophie watched Alain's mother and daughter head down the steps and across the square, then turned back to find Marjolaine, her long French braid swinging down her back, moving toward the far end of the room, where dusty purple drapes were drawn across the stage. She stopped with one hand on the back of an aisle seat and looked up at the plaster ceiling. "As far as I can see, the stain isn't spreading. That's a good sign, but it's really hard to tell unless you're up in the attic. The stairway is backstage. It's narrow and steep and gives me the willies every time I climb it."

"Is that how you get into the cupola? I've always wondered where the opening was. Maude would never show me when I was little. She was afraid it wasn't safe. I'll bet it's a great view from up there."

"It's one I'd like to see, as well." Both women turned at the sound of a masculine voice.

"Hello, Luc," Marjolaine said with a wave.

"I didn't expect to see you here," Sophie said.

"I'm delivering a message. Your mother wants you to call her and she says she hasn't been able to get you on your cell."

"That's because I let the battery run down. It's on the charger in my room. I'll call her from here."

"I don't believe it was anything urgent, but I told her I'd deliver the message since I was coming into town for dinner anyway."

"Thank you."

He placed one foot on the cross piece of an aisle seat and braced his hands on his thigh. He looked up at the ceiling just as the two women had done moments earlier. "How's the patch holding?" he asked Marjolaine.

"Pretty well, I think. I was just telling Sophie that you really need to be up in the attic to tell. And I'm not going up there today. It's far too dark and dreary and I don't have a key. I'll get Alain to check it out tomorrow or the next day if you're going to be here working. Is that all right?"

Sophie hoped her color wasn't rising. "Yes, of course. He can stop by anytime. As a matter of fact, I need to talk to him. I can't find the code to the alarm system anywhere in Maude's things. I'm hoping, she gave him a copy to keep at the police station."

"Why don't you ask him now?" Luc straightened, resting his hands on the back of the seat. "I just saw him going into the Blue Moon with his mother and little girl. Would you two ladies care to join me there? Marjo can fill us in on the Acadian music festival the Indigo Development Committee's hoping to hold here in October."

"Here in the building?" Sophie asked, gazing around at the overcrowded space. It was the first she'd heard of a music festival.

"That would be great, of course," Marjolaine said hastily. "But we never got around to getting Maude's permission. The most we were hoping for was that she'd let us give tours of the building during the weekend of the festival. Our goal, in partnership with the historical society, is to eventually buy the opera house, restore it and use it as the staging area for zydeco and Cajun music festivals. Sort of a mini Grand Ole Opry." She looked around, a frown pulling her strongly marked brows together. "Maude was our buffer. As long as Past Perfect was a going concern, we figured the owner wouldn't sell the building out from under us…the town, I mean. Now we have no idea what will happen to it."

"The lease is up at the end of the year."

"We know. That's why we need the festival to be a success. So we have funds on hand when we start negotiating with the owner. We're having a planning meeting next week. We'd love for you to come."

"I'll try," Sophie said. "But I don't know if I can even reopen Past Perfect without a trustworthy manager. I have responsibilities to fulfill the bequests in Maude's will. It might mean liquidating the business as soon as possible. There might not be enough money to keep up the lease for almost a year."

Marjolaine's lips thinned. "Then that's something else we'll have to consider."

"I'm sorry." Sophie felt miserable, but didn't know what else she could do to help at the moment.

"We can't do anything more about it this afternoon," Marjo said. "I have to be going." She turned to Luc. "Thanks for the dinner invitation, Luc, but my brother's expecting me home. I'll take a rain check, though."

He smiled. "I'll hold you to that."

"See ya'll later," Marjo said and headed back out into the rain.

"Oh dear," Sophie said. "I'm afraid she's unhappy with me."

"She'll get over it. To tell you the truth, it's a long shot that the town will be able to come up with the money for this white elephant anyway. It'll cost an arm and a leg to restore it. And the upkeep's going to be a bitch."

"But it would be a real asset to the town. Think of the tourist dollars it would bring in. Indigo's right on the Evangeline Trail. It could be a real draw."

"Let's discuss it over dinner. Maybe there's some way to work it out. I know it's a little early but Willis's gumbo never lasts long."

She hesitated then decided to accept his invitation. She'd probably be eating at the Blue Moon anyway and it would be pleasant to have company. "I'd like that. I skipped lunch, so an early dinner suits me just fine. If you give me a minute to call my mother and make sure everything's all right back home, I'll join you there."

"ESTELLE, come here." Cecily poked her head inside the kitchen door of the diner. She'd told Alain she was going to the bathroom. Luckily the hallway that led to the restrooms also led to the kitchen so she could talk to Estelle and Willis without Alain seeing her.

Estelle turned away from the huge restaurant stove, where a big stainless-steel pot of gumbo steamed, and waved a distracted hand. "Not now, Cecily. I'm swamped with orders."

Willis was working the grill. "How's it going, Cecily?" He lifted his spatula in a salute, but didn't lift his eyes from the row of burgers and crawfish cakes sizzling on the hot surface.

"Fine, Willis. And yourself?" You didn't skip the pleasantries in Indigo, no matter what else was on your mind.

"I've had worse days." He'd lost a lot of weight fighting his cancer, but he no longer had that pinched look to his face, and the grayness that underlay his dark skin had disappeared.

"Glad to hear it. Now, Estelle, we need to talk." She spoke the words sharply. The diner was almost full. Someone could come walking down the hall at any moment, including her own son, the Chief of Police. It had been a half hour since she'd stolen the little teddy, marked with the double purple diamond on the price tag that was the code for Willis's cancer med, but she was still shaking. She'd barely been able to swallow her dinner, she was so upset.

Estelle wiped her hands on the apron around her waist and turned away from the pot of gumbo. She crossed the big, steamy kitchen as Cecily eased inside the swinging door. "What is it, Cecily? You look as if you've seen a ghost come up out of the bayou."

"I have Willis's meds." She looked over her shoulder at the door, expecting to see Alain bearing down on her. Imagine the headlines in the *Parish Gazette* if she should be arrested by her own son. It didn't bear thinking of.

"You what?" Estelle's eyes widened. "Did I hear you right?"

"You heard me." Cecily fumbled in her bag and pulled out the little teddy. "Quick, get something to hide it in before someone else sees it."

A big smile broke out on Estelle's care-worn face as she studied the price tag with its distinctive marking. "Thank God. We were about ready to get in the car and drive to Canada ourselves to get some more. How did you get your hands on it? Did she give you the rest of them?"

"She didn't give me anything," Cecily hissed. "I stole it, may God forgive me." She made the sign of the cross, then went on to explain as quickly as she could what had happened. While she talked, Estelle lifted a stainless-steel container down from a shelf.

"No one will look for it there. It'll be safe until we close up for the night. So you couldn't get any of the others?"

"No." Cecily shook her head. It had all happened so quickly. She still couldn't believe she'd had the nerve to take the teddy at all, but when it fell on the floor and bounced away from the others, she'd taken advantage of the situation and slipped it into her purse.

"The Lord will forgive you," Estelle said, blinking away a tear. "And Willis and I do surely bless you."

"Thanks. But we need more than a blessing. We need a miracle. We can't keep going in there and snatching them piecemeal this way. We need to get them all at once. Oh, I wish she hadn't seen them."

"What if she puts them out for sale?" Estelle asked, her eyes widening. "I mean, she must have commented on the price." She looked down at the little bear. "He's cute and all...but..."

"I'm worried about that, too." They ordered the drugs through a pharmacy in Nova Scotia close to her cousin's home. All seventeen members of their group paid individually for the meds, most by credit card, and then gave her cousin's home as the shipping address. Cecily's cousin sewed the meds into the stuffed toys she loved to make and sent them across the border in monthly shipments. It had been Maude's idea to have her put the prices of the drugs on the tags she attached to the animals along with an identifying code of squares and triangles. Never any names. When each of the members of the group came to collect their animal, she matched their invoices with the tags and their colored code. Cecily had never felt it was a foolproof system, but since Maude had been willing to be the one to accept the smuggled shipments, she'd never felt as if she could voice her misgivings.

And happily her cousin was a very meticulous woman. In over two years there hadn't been a single mix-up, so maybe Maude's system was a good one.

"I wish we'd known she was going back to Houston like she did," Estelle said, breaking into her thoughts as she dropped the teddy bear into the metal canister and covered it with the bag of brown sugar. "Maybe we could have gotten in—"

"It's too late now for that. She's seen them. She'll know they're gone now even if we're lucky enough to get in and out of the opera house without being caught. Sophie's no fool. She'll remember what happened today. I don't want her to think I'm a shoplifter." A horrible thought struck her. "Or that Dana stole it. She was with me when I took Willis's bear but I made sure she didn't see me put it in my purse. Lord, what have I done?"

"The right thing," Estelle assured her.

"I don't suppose we could wait until she puts them out on the shelf and then all go in and buy them back," Cecily said hopefully.

Estelle's lips drew into a straight line. "These drugs are so expensive already. But—"

Cecily waved her off. "I know. I know. It was just a thought."

"If worse comes to worst we'll tell her the truth," Estelle said.

"I don't want Alain to find out what we're up to." She had to consider the fact that he wanted to run for parish sheriff in the future, but Cecily had also noticed the way he'd looked at Sophie when she came into the Blue Moon with Luc Carter. Alain still cared for her. No one else might have noticed, but she was his mother and she knew. How could he ever have any kind of relationship with her if his own mother was convicted of stealing from her?

"Order up," Marie called out. She was filling in for Estelle and Willis's regular waitress for a couple of days while she recovered from an abscessed tooth. Whatever bad you could say about Marie Lesatz—and there was a lot, to Cecily's way of thinking—she had a good heart. Always ready to help a friend even when she spent eight hours a night on her feet. She spied Cecily in the kitchen and turned her head to call over her shoulder. "Hey, Alain. I found your mom. She didn't faint in the bathroom, so don't worry. She's in the kitchen with Estelle."

Time had run out. Cecily looked at Estelle and then at Marie. "I'm going to talk to my mom. But are you thinking what I'm thinking?"

Estelle sighed, then nodded. "If there's any one of us that can figure out how to get in and out of Past Perfect without getting caught, it's Marie."

CHAPTER EIGHT

THE SUN was shining for the first time in almost a week, so Alain left the SUV in his parking space behind the city building and headed out on foot. Indigo didn't have much of a business district anymore. As in small towns all over the country, there were more empty storefronts than going concerns, but those that remained, the general store—really a combination grocery and convenience store—the hardware, the drugstore, an auto-parts store, the diner and a combination flower and gift shop, were well cared for and holding their own.

The air was unseasonably warm and a couple of elderly gentlemen were sitting on the benches beneath the war memorial, smoking and shooting the breeze. Bart Lafever and his brother-in-law sunning themselves in the square was as sure a sign of spring as the swallows returning to Capistrano. The drugstore windows were filled with red, white and pink Valentine cutouts and the hardware had a display of small appliances and red candy heart boxes to remind husbands and boyfriends that a toaster oven, too, was a gift of love. Estelle and Willis had a sandwich board out in front of the Blue Moon advertising a surf-and-turf special for the holiday with crème brûlée featured as dessert. Willis must be feeling better if he was firing up the blow torch for crème brûlée.

Alain hooked his thumbs in his utility belt and made a mental note to pick up a rose each for his mother and grandmother. Since he didn't have a sweetheart to buy for, Valentine's Day tended to slip his mind, or would, if Dana didn't have the dining-room table littered with dozens of Dora the Explorer valentines for her class-mates.

Another week had gone by and he still hadn't con-nected with Casey Jo. He was beginning to hope she'd lost interest in the trip to Disney World. Dana still jumped up to answer the phone every time it rang, but she'd stopped pestering him about the trip. Maybe, this once, it would all blow over, but knowing his ex-wife as he did, he doubted it.

He touched a finger to the brim of his hat as he passed a pair of his grandmother's cronies entering the drug-store. "Afternoon, Miss Lillian, Miss Sarah. Nice day, isn't it?"

They returned the greeting, stopping to ask after Yvonne, and he promised to pass on their hellos. That exchange was followed by five minutes of discussion of the weather, and the fact that it was getting too warm, too early in the year. Meant a bad tornado season in their experience, which between them, Alain guessed, added up to about a hundred and sixty years or so. The conversation concluded with both elderly women holding to their faith in the Good Lord and keeping their TVs tuned to the Weather Channel to see them through.

The radio receiver on his shoulder crackled to life, giving him an excuse to move on down the street without seeming impolite for cutting the visit short. It was only a reminder from his dispatcher that he had a five-thirty meeting with the mayor to go over the department budget requests for the next quarter, and not an emergency call, but it served.

He continued on his way, skirting the square, swinging over a block on Jefferson, passing by Maude Picard's house, wondering what Sophie planned to do with it. He cut back across the square, arrived at the opera house and tried the door. It was unlocked so he walked inside, buttoning his sunglasses into his shirt pocket as he waited for his eyes to adjust to the dimness. Sophie was nowhere in sight. The doors to the auditorium were standing open and he heard the foot-tapping sounds of zydeco coming from the stage.

She'd been busy the past few days, he noticed. Guy and two of his friends from the high-school football team had helped her sort through and move all the inventory in the auditorium so it would be accessible to the appraiser. His son had told him all about it as they'd shared a pizza the night before.

There was some cool stuff in there, Guy had continued, warming to the subject. Like an entire steamer trunk full of old clothes. Mostly women's stuff, he said, but there was also a Civil War uniform jacket and sword. "I'll bet it's worth a lot of money," his son had speculated. "But Sophie says it should be in a museum." Alain agreed and was pleased Sophie felt the same way.

Since Guy had broached the subject, Alain let

himself pose a question or two. "How was Sophie to work for?" he'd asked casually as he helped himself to another slice of pepperoni-laden pizza, figuring he'd take a handful of antacids before he went to bed to ward off the inevitable heartburn.

It had been hard work, Guy admitted. Most of that old furniture weighed a ton. But Sophie was easy to work for, and a generous employer. She'd brought a cooler of bottled water and sodas, and didn't get all hyper when Willis and Estelle's grandson, Antoine, dropped a couple of plates and broke them. "She said they weren't all that valuable and she didn't even dock his pay or anything." Guy had a goofy smile on his face and an unfocused look in his eye as he talked about Sophie.

"That was nice of her." Alain suspected his son had a little bit of a crush on her. Hell, he'd start to worry if he didn't, a woman as good-looking and sexy as Sophie Clarkson.

His thoughts of the evening before had carried him into the middle of the auditorium, but Sophie wasn't anywhere around. The music was coming from a boom box on the stage, one the size of a carry-on bag and easy to spot. The acoustics were good in the old building and the sound carried to where he was standing, even though the volume wasn't tuned very high. Half a dozen books were lying on tables and the tops of dressers. He tilted his head to read the titles: *Throwaway Treasures. The Amateur Guide to Antebellum Antiques. American Furniture of the Eighteenth and Nineteenth Century. A Guide to Southern Antiquing.* The books were marked with dozens of strips of colored paper. Sophie was obviously doing her homework. For a moment he let himself hope that meant she was going to stay in Indigo. But only for a moment. *Get a grip,* he told himself. Sophie Clarkson was a successful fund-raiser with a life and career in Houston. She wasn't a small-town girl. Never had been. Never would be.

"Oh dear, is that you, Alain?" Her words came floating down from somewhere above him. He zeroed in on the bow-fronted box to the left of the stage.

"I'm here to take a look at the patch on the roof. Marjolaine told me you knew I'd be stopping by."

"I lost track of the time." There was embarrassed laughter in her tone. She appeared in the box, leaning her arms on the gilded railing. "You caught me playing dress-up."

Alain sucked in his breath. She was wearing something white and sheer, all lace and tiny tucks. *Ye gods, was it a corset?* Her shoulders were bare, and so were the rounded tops of her breasts. A huge straw hat bedecked with pale-pink roses and what appeared to be ostrich plumes framed her face and tied under her chin with a lacy bow. She'd twisted her hair up under the hat, or tried to, but her hair had always had a mind of its own, and here and there stray curls shimmered against her cheeks and neck in sunlight that was filled with dancing dust motes.

She lifted one hand to her throat. "This is awkward," she said. "I'm up here and my clothes are down there." She leaned a little forward to point to her jeans and sweater set draped over the back of one of the chairs in the row ahead of him.

"I'm a cop," he said, hoping his voice didn't crack with the strain of keeping himself from getting hard. "I noticed that first thing."

Her cheeks were as pink as the roses that adorned the preposterous hat and she looked...? He didn't know how to describe the way she looked. His brain had shut down. Her eyes widened in alarm and she leaned slightly forward to look over his shoulder to the open doorway. "There's no one else with you, is there?"

"I'm alone," he assured her. "Want me to bring your things up to you?" *And then lie down on the floor and make love with you?* That's what he wanted to do so bad he could almost taste it.

She hesitated a moment, her color going a little deeper, as though she might have had the same wayward thought. "No." She gave her head a little shake as she straightened. "I'll come down."

She disappeared behind the side wall of the box and a moment later materialized at the top of the staircase. She was indeed wearing a corset and a floor-length petticoat of pale ivory silk and yellowing lace that swirled around her legs when she walked. The corset followed the flare of her hips, narrowing to a point just above the juncture of her thighs. His heart started hammering in his chest and he realized he'd been holding his breath. He let it out with a whoosh. There were too many layers of silk and lace to tell what she was wearing beneath the petticoats, but it couldn't be much. Her jeans were lying underneath her sweater. It wasn't because he was a cop that he'd noticed the wispy blue bra on top of the pile. And it definitely wasn't a cop that reasoned if the bra was pale-blue and wispy, so were the panties that matched it.

She halted at the foot of the stairs a good two yards away from him. "I found these in a trunk yesterday. I…I couldn't resist trying them on." She touched the delicate ruffle of lace that lay against her breast with the tip of her finger. "They're like something from a Victorian Victoria's Secret, don't you think?"

Alain shifted uncomfortably. At this rate he was going to need a cold shower when he got out of here.

"Then I heard something up in the balcony," she said. "I thought a squirrel, or maybe a cat, or heaven help us, a skunk had gotten shut up in here and I went to look."

He couldn't stop staring at her, and she wasn't so embarrassed she didn't notice.

"Alain, your mouth's hanging open."

He got his jaw muscles back under control and closed his mouth. Her legs were long for her height and he remembered how she'd wrapped them around him when they had made love. She leaned forward to grab her sweater, and hurriedly pushed the bra out of sight. She whirled the sweater around her shoulders and the creamy swells of her breasts vanished from view. Alain felt like a kid who'd just discovered coal in his Christmas stocking.

"As I was saying, we found this entire steamer trunk of vintage clothes yesterday when Guy and his friends were helping me get ready for the appraiser." She looked down, smoothing her hands over the layers of silk and lace. When she raised her face to his, her eyes shone with the excitement of a little girl playing dress-up. "I've always wondered what it would feel like wearing a corset. I couldn't resist trying it on."

"How does it feel?" he asked.

She laid her hand on her stomach. "The stays are bone, probably whalebone, and they poke something fierce. I can't breathe and I can't bend over." She smiled. "And I didn't even lace it tightly. The material's too fragile, and well, frankly, I'm too fat."

"You aren't fat." As far as he was concerned she was just right. He let his eyes travel over the utterly feminine curves of her body. The tips of her running shoes peeked out from under the embroidered hem of the petticoat, but he found even that anachronism sexy.

"Thank you," she said. "But I'm fatter than the woman this corset was made for. At least in the waist... and other places."

"I noticed that, too," he said before he could stop himself.

"I noticed you noticed." She fell silent, but when he didn't take the hint and move, she said, "If you'll excuse me, I'll change now."

"Oh. Sure." He shoved the brim of his Stetson up then stopped himself from running his finger under his uniform collar. Either the temperature in the room had gone up twenty degrees, or his had. "I'll wait for you on the stage." They hadn't made love in more than fifteen years. He hadn't even kissed her, or held her, or touched her since the day Casey Jo had found them in this very spot, but his body remembered and the blood ran like lava through his veins.

"I'll only be a moment."

"Take your time." He pivoted, got his legs moving, and took two steps, but she called him back.

"Alain?"

He almost groaned out loud. He turned his head. She was holding the sweater against her, the roses in her cheeks brighter than before. "Yeah?"

"I... There's a knot." She turned her back and looked at him over her shoulder, a Victorian temptress in lace and silk and a ridiculous hat that was about the sexiest get-up he'd ever seen. There was real distress in her eyes. "I...don't want to break the lacing."

He walked toward her on wooden legs. He could see her spine between the edges of the corset. He remembered, suddenly, the way she'd shivered under his hands when he touched her there, just above the swell of her buttocks. He felt himself grow hard thinking about the softness of her skin beneath his fingers. To clamp down on his thoughts and his libido, he stared at a tiny mole on her shoulder.

"How did you get it on?" he asked as he fumbled with the knot in the woven lacing. Too late he realized what her answer would be. Up close he could smell lavender, old and faded like the material, and beneath it her scent, warm and womanly, and overlying it all the mundane odor of moth balls. He forced himself to concentrate on the mothballs as he worked.

"I—" she straightened her shoulders a bit, as though she too might be steeling herself against the brush of his fingers "—I laced it up the front and turned it around, but I pulled the strings too tightly to undo it that way."

He steeled himself against the effect of that mental image on certain excitable parts of his anatomy as he worked at the knot.

Once he loosened the lacing, she spun around so quickly he felt the swirl of silk against his pant leg. "The petticoats have hooks and eyes. I think I can manage them on my own."

"We're good to go, then," he said. He took off once more for the stage, taking deep breaths, telling himself it had just been too long since he'd been that close to a half-naked woman.

But he was only fooling himself. It wasn't just any half-naked woman back there. It was Sophie Clarkson. His first love, and he'd be telling a bald-faced lie if he said he didn't want her back in his arms, in his bed and in his life.

CHAPTER NINE

HER HANDS were still shaking as she folded the corset and petticoat and laid them on the horsehair fainting couch that she'd had Guy and his buddies move out of the main aisle to a spot under the balcony staircase. She'd spent two hours on the Internet trying to track down its origins when she couldn't find one like it in any of the reference books Maude had kept stashed under the counter. She smiled a little as she sat down to tie her shoes. She'd finally come across the description of one similar in many respects on an obscure Web site devoted to handmade reproductions. She wasn't one-hundred-percent certain—she'd have to rely on the appraiser's opinion—but if the markings on the underside were authentic, Maude had picked up a gem of an antebellum piece, hand-carved by slave labor on a Mississippi plantation known for its furniture-making.

She would have to contact one of the big dealers in New Orleans or Houston to see if they would take it on commission or maybe put it up for auction. She'd probably get enough for it to pay the appraiser's fee if the bidding went high enough.

She gave the corset a final pat and started up the aisle

toward the stage. She couldn't believe she'd given in to the temptation to try the darned thing on when she'd known Alain would be dropping by to check on the roof sometime that afternoon. Or had she hoped he might find her in it?

Of course not, she told herself sternly. It had merely been the natural curiosity of a twenty-first-century woman to experience what her great-great-grandmother had endured in the name of fashion. As for Alain showing up, she'd simply lost track of time, that was all. And now that she thought about it, oddly enough, she hadn't felt oppressed by the constrictions of the garment. She'd felt, well, feminine, sexy and alluring.

"That's because you didn't lace up tightly enough to feel oppressed," she scolded herself.

"Did you say something?" Alain stretched out a hand to help her up the set of steep narrow steps to the stage.

"Just talking to myself." When she was safely on the apron, he dropped down on his haunches and began looking through the stack of tapes and the few CDs she'd found, along with the decade-old boom box in one of Maude's filing cabinets.

Alain held up a CD. "Beausoleil. Good stuff. Classic zydeco." Sophie liked the foot-tapping music but it wasn't something she sought out unless she was in Indigo.

"Ever listen to these guys?" He popped the lid on the boom box, to place the CD inside. "Indigo Boneshakers."

"Local?" she asked, looking down on him. He'd taken off the Stetson and laid it at the edge of the stage.

His dark-brown hair glinted with chestnut highlights, and as far as she could tell, it was as thick as it had been when he was younger. Her fingers itched to reach out and feel for herself if it was still as soft as she remembered.

"Yeah, a couple of the guys are. My dispatcher Billy Paul Exeter's the drummer. The rest are from Lafayette and around." Alain pushed the Play button and the music started again. "This album's pure Cajun, but these guys play everything from zydeco to Elvis. I sit in with them now and then when they need a fiddle player."

"Why didn't you follow your dream and try and make it in the music business?" she asked.

He shrugged. "Life happened. I grew up fast after we broke up."

"It took me a lot longer," she said, thinking of her carefree college days, the whirlwind of parties that followed her engagement to Randall, the fairy-tale wedding. And the divorce that had sent her running back to Indigo and into Alain's arms.

He was following his own train of thought. His voice was low and quiet, whiskey-rough, as it rasped across her nerve endings. "It was the right thing to do, Sophie. Letting you go."

She sighed. She'd been hurt and disappointed but she hadn't been ready for marriage and they both knew it. "I had my way to find, too." She thought of her failed marriage and her own unfulfilled dreams of a home and children. "I just wish I hadn't taken a wrong turn along the way."

"You and me both."

"You have Guy and Dana. Doesn't that make up for a lot of hurt?"

"They're my life. I'd like to believe becoming a husband and a father made me a man, but it was the army that did that. Working at the husband and father jobs came later. You might say I'm still a work in progress in that department."

He smiled the crooked grin that started at one corner of his mouth and worked its way across his face just as it had when he was young. But today it didn't quite reach his eyes.

"You gave up your dream for them," she said.

"That's all it was, Sophie, a boy's dream. I had a family to support on a cop's pay. There wasn't time for music. There still isn't, except now and then."

"No regrets?"

"Just one." Their eyes locked. Her heart began to beat a little faster. She knew he was talking about her and what they'd had and been too young to keep hold of. He stood up and the moment was broken. "We'd better head upstairs or we'll lose the light."

He held out his hand to help her up. Too much time had gone by to resurrect the past. Neither of them were kids anymore. It was impossible to rekindle what they'd felt for each other so long ago. Wasn't it?

"Here's the stairs," he said, leading her behind the stage. When she was little and had sneaked back here, it had always surprised her how light and airy the space was. The beadboard paneling was painted white and sunlight streamed in through three tall narrow windows along the back of the building. There were no dressing rooms, but long iron rods that had once held curtains, giving the actors some privacy for costume changes, still protruded from the walls, as well as rows of wrought-iron hooks for hanging street clothes and props. To her disappointment, then and now, none of those props or pieces of scenery remained. But if Marjolaine and Hugh were right, some of those relics might be right above her head.

Alain walked to the far end of the building to a door that Sophie didn't remember from her childhood. He pulled a key out of his pocket and fitted it into the deadbolt lock.

"Has this door always been here?" she asked. "I can't recall seeing it when I was little and searching for a way into the cupola."

"The stairway's always been here, but Maude kept the doorway boarded up and painted over. She figured it would keep teenagers from trying to climb up here. It was a pretty big deal, kind of a rite of passage in my granddad's day. She put a new door on after Katrina blew through and the workmen needed to be in and out of the attic to fix the roof."

"Why didn't she have it boarded up again when the roof was fixed? I'd think it would be just as much of a challenge to kids today as it was to your granddad."

"Hugh Prejean and some of the others asked her not to. Besides, I'd taken over the chief's job by then and she figured her tax money was paying for me to keep vandals off the property." An equal mixture of exasperation and amusement underscored his words.

Sophie smiled, too. "That sounds like something she would say."

Alain unhooked a flashlight from his belt. "Ready? It's darker than Hades up here. No electricity."

Once more he offered his hand, and this time Sophie was ready for the tiny frisson of awareness his touch produced. The stairs were narrow and steep, but when they stood at the top she gasped in surprise. Most of the big room was in shadow, but directly under the cupola was a pool of muted sunlight. The floor was covered in wide-planked cypress and seemed sturdy enough. Alain must have thought so, because he strode off without any hesitation, shining the flashlight up into the rafters.

As her eyes adjusted to the dimness, Sophie lost interest in the condition of the roof. All around her were piles and piles of…treasure, just as Marjolaine had said. Old sign boards announcing the appearance of Vaudeville acts and minstrel shows, oil lanterns that looked as if they must be the original stage lighting, a huge roll of canvas that would have taken half a dozen men to carry up those narrow stairs. A thought struck her. "Alain, is that what I think it is?"

He turned around, the flashlight beam sliding across the floor in front of him, illuminating a stack of painted scenery portraying a scene that could only be Venice and must have been the backdrop of a century-old production of Shakespeare or perhaps an Italian opera. "I know exactly what it is," he said, shining his light on the canvas, and she heard amusement in his voice. "It's the original stage curtain from downstairs."

"What's it doing up here? I mean, it's valuable. Maybe irreplaceable."

He came over and dropped onto his haunches beside her. "It's only irreplaceable to those of us who live here in Indigo." He reached out and poked the big, heavy roll with his flashlight. "It's up here because it's too far gone to restore. Maude and the others were just trying to keep it from deteriorating any further. They were hoping to be able to recreate it…if they ever got the money."

"It still should be stored somewhere with better climate control and where mice and bugs can't get at it."

"You're beginning to sound like an antique dealer."

"It's a piece of history," she said indignantly, but she did feel as if she'd made a rare discovery. It was a feeling she never had wining and dining prospective university donors for Clarkson and Hillman, and never would, she thought with a pang.

"Probably," he said. "But you're forgetting technically it belongs to the owner of the building. Some Canadian guy who isn't interested in the place beyond the revenue it brings in."

She looked around. "How sad. Those boxes are probably more of the opera-house records. They need to be stored correctly, too. There's a lot of history here."

"There is." He held out his hand and Sophie's heart skipped a beat or two as she took it. So much for telling herself they could be comfortable together, just old friends. It wasn't working. At least not for her. "We'd better get back downstairs."

She willed her stuttering heart back into rhythm and stood up, but the octagonal pool of sunlight beckoned. Within its radius a narrow, ladderlike stairway led to an equally narrow catwalk beneath the cupola windows. "I may never get back up here. I'd like to see the view from the skylight. It must be marvelous. Can you spare a minute or two before we go back downstairs?"

"Sure. I haven't been in the attic since after Katrina and Rita, and then it was to wrestle half a dozen sheets of plywood up here to board up the broken windows. The view wasn't all that great then." His face darkened as he thought back to those dark days. "But I'll bet it is today."

"Who paid to replace the broken glass?" she asked as she mounted the rusty metal treads. She was very conscious of Alain behind her as she stepped onto the catwalk, his heat, his scent, his bulk.

"Insurance. The landlord may be absentee but he's conscientious. He keeps plenty of insurance on the building."

She leaned her hands on the sill of one of the narrow windows that ringed the copper-roofed cupola and looked out over the Bayou Teche, brown-green and sluggish as it flowed behind the building. She knew that the old Valois plantation had once sat on the high ground on the far shore, but it had burned to the ground sometime in the early nineteen hundreds and nothing remained of the house or outbuildings. The land had been sold off in pieces even before that time, if she remembered Maude's rambling history lessons. "Do you suppose it looked like Shadows-on-the-Teche?" she asked, referring to the famous restored plantation house not many miles away in New Iberia where Maude had taken her as a child.

"What?" Alain asked, turning toward her. He had moved to the front of the skylight and was looking down over the town square.

Sophie hid her smile. A cop first, last and always, he was observing his domain, not dreaming of hoop-skirted belles and dashing cavalry officers with swords at their sides.

"The old Valois plantation. Do you think it was as beautiful as Shadows-on-the-Teche?"

"I doubt it," he said. "It was a big house for these parts but nothing to compare to Shadows. I don't know if there are any pictures of the place still in existence. I'll ask my grandmother. She was a Valois, you know. A poor relation of the original family. The land-owning Valois immigrated to Canada after Reconstruction. The only one ever to come back was Amelie, Alexandre Valois's widow. She's buried beside him in St. Timothy's cemetery."

"I know that part of the story. Growing up, I thought it was the most romantic thing in the world that she came back here and died at his graveside."

"Funny, I always thought it was a foolish trip for a sick old woman to make in the dead of winter."

She wrinkled her nose. "Just like a man." She picked out the angel that crowned the white marble Valois vault standing above all the others in the church cemetery. "No romance in your soul. You can quote all the facts you want, but I'll always believe she clung to life until she could be reunited with her lost love. Indigo's own Evangeline and Gabriel."

"You'll have to write up the story for the tourists. Too bad no one's ever claimed to see or hear their ghosts in here. That would be a real draw."

"If Amelie was going to haunt somewhere, this would be the perfect place. Maude said she had a beautiful voice."

"So I've always heard."

She turned her head and found him watching her. She took a step away from him because he was standing too close and she liked it.

"Be careful or you'll fall over the railing," he cautioned.

Since the railing was only knee-high she did as he told her. "Is that your mother's house?" she asked, pointing toward Lafayette Street.

"Yep," he said. "And there's my grandmother's place two streets over."

"This is a marvelous view," she said, her gaze resting first on the Blue Moon Diner and then the Savoy Funeral Home. She let her eyes follow the river's meandering path out the Bayou Road toward La Petite Maison. Thinking of Luc's establishment brought her back to a sense of time and place. "Oh dear," she said aloud. "What time is it? I promised Luc I'd be back for tea this afternoon. He's serving some new pastries that Loretta Castille baked this morning. He's booked for the weekend and I gather he wants to make a good impression on the new guests."

He leaned closer. The sunlight beat down around

them, soft and warming as it filtered through the glass. "Don't let your heart overrule your good judgment where Carter is concerned."

"I'm not," she said. "Not that it's any of your business what I do with my heart."

He lifted his hand to touch her hair, brushing it back behind her ear. "I know that. It's my redneck, school-of-hard-knocks way of asking if you're sweet on him?"

"That's none of your business, either," she said, but it took a lot of effort to get the words past the sudden constriction in her throat.

"I'm asking because I don't go around kissing women who are interested in other men."

"Kissing?" Her heart thundered in her ears as the blood rushed to her head.

"Yes, kissing." He reached out and cupped the back of her neck with his big, rough hand. He leaned in just enough to brush his lips over hers. Except for his hand on the back of her neck, it was the only place their bodies touched. She found it surprisingly erotic, surprisingly arousing. "I've wanted to do this ever since I saw you in front of Savoy's that night in the rain, with Carter holding that big umbrella and standing too damned close to suit me."

"I told…"

"I know." The brush of his lips grew bolder as he tilted her head back. Her lips parted, almost as though they had a mind of their own. She reached up, wrapped her hands around his neck, arched her back so that her breasts brushed against his shirtfront. She could feel the outline of his shield through the thin cotton of her sweater.

The badge was the symbol of his duty and responsibility to Indigo. The duties and responsibilities of a man, not a boy. And his mouth was a man's mouth. His hands a man's hands. There was nothing of the boy she had once been infatuated with in his touch or in his kiss, but there were echoes of the younger man who had recaptured her heart, at least for a little while, seven summers ago.

Sophie stiffened at the unwanted memory of Casey Jo bursting in on them.

Alain lifted his head. His eyes were the same dark blue as the bayou sky before a summer storm. "What's wrong?" he asked. He brushed a tumbled fall of curls behind her ear. "Don't tell me you didn't like it, because I'd know you were lying."

"I liked it." She pressed her lips together. They still tingled from the pressure of his mouth against hers, her body still thrummed with the stirrings of the kind of passion she hadn't felt in, oh so long.

"But you were remembering the last time we kissed in this building." He drew his thumb across her cheek and then dropped his hand, taking a step back, giving her space.

She nodded. Words had deserted her.

"Casey Jo and I have been divorced for almost four years, separated a year before that. Ever since she took off and left Guy in tears and Dana still in diapers to try her luck at being a Vegas showgirl." His voice was flat, a parody of normal, but the humiliation he tried to hide betrayed itself in his storm-dark eyes. "It was the last straw for me, Sophie. I filed for divorce the next day."

"It's not about Casey Jo," she said. "Or at least only partly. You said it yourself. She's still a part of your life and always will be because you have children together. But it's about me, too. I'm not the same person I was before. I have a life and a career in Houston. I...I don't belong in Indigo. I probably never did." But could she now? Could she leave all she'd worked for behind and become part of this small, insular town? She didn't know, and at the moment she was afraid to think of trying.

She was trembling. Her hands were shaking and her stomach was all tied up in knots. Her response to him had been even stronger than she'd anticipated. What was left between them? Something more than she wanted to acknowledge? Something that would set her life spinning off down a different path than the one she'd been following?

"We're getting into pretty deep waters after only one kiss," he said.

She dared to look in his eyes once more and saw that the passion that had burned in them moments before had been banked. Now the blue depths reflected only her own confusion. "Yes, we are. It's probably just leftover psychic energy, or old vibes, or something." She tried for a lighter note and almost made it.

He reached out and touched her lips with the pad of his thumb. "Or something," he echoed, and the words sent another shiver rippling over her skin.

Or something. Like love?

CHAPTER TEN

SOPHIE SHIFTED a little in her seat. Her bottom was starting to go numb. The midmorning meeting of the combined Indigo Historical Society and the festival planning group had been going on for over an hour in the private dining room at the rear of the Blue Moon Diner and now threatened to drag on into the noon hour. To give her credit, Marjolaine Savoy had kept the dozen or so Indigo citizens on topic, ruthlessly wielding her power as chairman to cut off what threatened to be a contentious debate on whether it was overreaching to stage a parade on the day of the festival, or if there was any possibility of adding a gala fireworks display in the evening.

The consensus was that the parade was a viable option, but the fireworks were too expensive. The service groups in town had already pledged money for the Fourth of July celebration and probably wouldn't want to sponsor another one so soon. But it wouldn't hurt to get their two cents' worth in for next year, Doc Landry had said before he was called away to look in on the mayor's ninety-year-old mother-in-law, who was having chest pains. Or indigestion, the crotchety doctor had grumbled on his way out the door. It was his opinion that Delia Larouche would outlive them all.

At that point Sophie had to look down at her hands to hide a smile. She'd met the good doctor once or twice since Maude's funeral and liked him, despite the perpetual scowl he wore. She had no trouble seeing through the gruff exterior to the caring, dedicated man beneath. What she did find hard to imagine was that in his younger days Mick Landry had played the *frottoir,* or rub-board—a musical instrument that consisted of a piece of corrugated sheet metal affixed to the chest with handles that fit over the shoulders. It was strummed—that was the only word Sophie could think of to describe it—with a thimble or some type of kitchen object and produced a sound that was uniquely Cajun.

Sophie's short talk on ways the committees could go about improving their fund-raising capabilities had been well received, and although she'd been reluctant when Marjolaine first asked for her input a day or two earlier, she'd enjoyed giving it. She hadn't told them much they couldn't have figured out for themselves. Grant money was probably available, but professional grant writers were expensive, although they should consider that outlay of funds if and when they did secure title to the opera house. For the immediate future, though, a direct-mail campaign to area residents and members of other historical groups whose mailing lists were available would probably bring in enough pledges to make the expense worthwhile; talks to area service groups would be enhanced with a slide-show presentation; the Indigo cookbook and CajunFest T-shirt sales had already repaid their initial outlay of funds and could also be used as radio-spot giveaways and advertising bonuses. Basic stuff. She finished by saying she would be more than happy to help in any way she could, as long as she was in Indigo, and once she returned to Houston, she would stay in touch. She sat down to a nice round of applause and the meeting moved on.

She spent a considerable amount of time in meetings with her clients in her work at Clarkson and Hillman, but few were as enjoyable as this one, she realized, even if it had gone on a bit. There had been energy and enthusiasm and a willingness to work hard to promote Indigo. It contrasted strongly with the staid and convention-bound milieu of corporate fund-raising.

Following up on the slide-show presentation suggestion, Hugh Prejean volunteered to search the library archives for old photographs of the opera house and its environs, and someone else offered to photograph some of the old play bills in the attic. But that idea was tabled until they could check with a lawyer and find out if that would be infringing on some right or other of the absentee owner of the opera house.

"What he don't know won't hurt him," a woman Sophie had never met grumbled. "Doesn't pay two hoots of attention to the place, anyway."

The meeting broke up shortly after that and the committee members filed out into the main seating area of the restaurant.

Honeycomb hearts in pink and red were suspended

on fishing line from the ceiling, clashing with the vintage green vinyl chairs and chrome tables that dated from the fifties. The floor was a checkerboard of black-and-white tiles. The countertop, where most of the regular lunch crowd chose to sit, was stainless steel, polished to a high sheen from years of being wiped down by two generations of waitresses. The room was crowded with diners filling up on the hearty lunch special of red beans and rice and homemade corn bread with a side salad of mixed greens and Willis's fabulous sweet-and-sour dressing.

Sophie saw an empty seat at the counter and decided to sit there. Willis Jefferson was at his usual place at the grill beyond the wide pass-through where orders were placed and picked up as he carried on a lively conversation with his patrons. She smiled a last goodbye to Marjolaine and turned to find Luc Carter arrowing in on the seat she'd been eyeing. He saw her at the same time and came to a halt. "Ladies first," he said gallantly.

"That's okay. I'll take the table by the window. It's empty."

"Are you sure? Counter seats are prime real estate in the Blue Moon."

"I'm aware of that," she said, laughing.

But while they'd been talking, the druggist, Byron McKee, had come in the back entrance and slid onto the low stool.

"Uh-oh," Luc said. "He who hesitates loses the counter seat."

"Join me at the table, then," Sophie offered. She had

seen little of her host the past several days. She'd had meetings with Maude's lawyer and her banker, tidying up the loose ends of the estate, and the rest of the time she'd spent at Past Perfect. For his part, Luc was busy with a house full of guests arriving for romantic Valentine's Day getaways. They were all friendly when she had met them in the dining room for breakfast, or on the porch for tea or cocktails, but they were all couples. And she was not.

She wondered if Luc felt the same?

He pulled out a chair for her and picked up the menu. "I'm having a burger and fries," he decided. "How about you?"

"The chicken breast salad with feta cheese and green grapes sounds delicious. I'll have that."

They gave their orders to the waitress and settled in to wait for their food. "How did the meeting go?" Luc asked. "I couldn't make it. I had a…business…appointment in Lafayette."

"Pretty well. Everyone's enthused and anxious to make it a success."

"That's half the battle. I've been thinking maybe we could work up some kind of walking tour of the town for the festival. What do you say to that?"

"I think that's a great idea. You should bring it up at the next meeting."

"I'll run it by Marjolaine, get her opinion."

Sophie filled him in on what had happened during the meeting. The efficient middle-aged waitress returned, served their food, refilled their sweet tea glasses and moved on to another table. Sophie speared a cube of chicken breast and raised it to her mouth. The fine hairs at the back of her neck stirred and she felt Alain's presence even before she saw him in the doorway of the diner. He was dressed in black as usual and, as usual, he made her heart skip a beat or two.

He didn't come directly to her. She hadn't expected him to. The people seated at the tables around them were his friends and neighbors, the citizens he had sworn to serve and protect. He greeted each of them with a half salute, or a wave and a friendly word.

"Carter," he said when he finally arrived at their table. "Shaping up to be a nice day."

"Supposed to be nice all weekend," Luc replied.

"Sophie." She suppressed a shiver of desire as the smoky heat of Alain's voice caressed her name.

"Hello, Alain." She hadn't seen him since their kiss in the cupola of the opera house two days earlier. She'd thought she had herself under control, that she would be ready for this, but she'd been wrong. She was trembling inside and out, and she couldn't stop herself from staring at his lips, remembering the feel of them against her own.

"How did the meeting go?" he asked, not quite ignoring Luc's presence, but coming close. "I got tied up on a 911 call."

"It went well. Luc and I were just discussing it. He couldn't make the meeting, either." She put her fork down so neither of them could see the slight tremor in her fingers. She'd been waiting for Alain to walk into the diner, she realized now. She'd been anticipating seeing him again ever since they'd climbed down out of the cupola and he'd walked off into the sunny afternoon. "They paged Dr. Landry out of the meeting," Sophie said. "Was that the call you were on?"

"Sam Castille's mother-in-law."

"I hope she's feeling better now," Sophie said.

"She's fine. Made herself a batch of jalapeño hush puppies and ate all of them. And then found out they didn't agree with her." He grinned and shook his head.

"Jalapeño hush puppies?"

"That's what she said."

"But she's ninety."

"Doesn't mean she doesn't still have an adventurous palate," Luc chimed in.

They all laughed at that, including Alain.

"I'm so glad she's all right," Sophie said, and she meant it. She had a host of acquaintances in Houston but only a few good friends, and all of them were busy with their own lives. They met for dinner or a movie now and then, but in between those events they went their separate ways. She was tired of being alone. She wanted to be part of a community. She wanted to gossip a little about her neighbors, worry about their health, rejoice in their successes. She wanted to belong.

"She's one tough old lady. She'll live to be a hundred, at least. I see Willis has my order ready. My dispatcher needs the afternoon off. It's my turn to man the barricades at the station."

"Here you are, Chief Boudreaux," Estelle said, coming out of the kitchen to hand him a plastic bag filled with carryout containers. "Annette'll ring you up at the register whenever you're ready to go."

"Thanks, Estelle." He accepted the bag with a smile then shifted his attention back to Sophie. "I finally got in touch with the company that installed the security system in the opera house. They're sending a technician out the first of the week to recalibrate it for you."

"Thanks, Alain, I appreciate that. The insurance company will be relieved to hear it, too. They're reluctant to let me open the store without it." She saw the surprise she'd anticipated at her announcement on Luc's handsome face, but Alain nodded as if he'd expected it all along.

"When did you make the decision to reopen Past Perfect? Or maybe I should be asking why?" Luc was watching her with those unreadable eyes of his.

"It's more or less an experiment. And I think it's what Maude would have wanted me to do." That conviction more than any other consideration had prompted her decision. "There's nine months left on the lease and tons, literally, of inventory. Hugh Prejean's niece, Amelia, has agreed to manage the store for me. She was one of Maude's best pickers, so she's qualified, and since she retired from teaching she's looking for something to do."

"You should have announced this news at the meeting," Luc told her. "They're all worried what the owner will do with the building if Past Perfect moves out."

"I thought I'd wait a few days to make a public announcement. I'll take out an advertisement in the *Parish Gazette,* maybe get one of those big banners to put across the front of the building."

Luc's smile grew wider at the enthusiasm in her

voice. Sophie glanced down at her plate in confusion. She shouldn't be so excited. It was only a temporary solution, as she'd just said. In a year, more than likely, Past Perfect would be…in the past. The realization jarred. When she looked up again she had her emotions under control.

"This way, everything should be running smoothly by the time I go back to Houston at the end of next week." She waited for Alain to respond to her statement but he said nothing. If she had been hoping to throw him off stride with her disclosure, she hadn't succeeded. At least not in any way that showed.

"We'll be sorry to see you go," Luc said politely.

"I've neglected my work there too long as it is."

"I understand."

But did Alain?

"I have to get back to the station. Let me know when the security tech shows up. I'll come right over." Alain touched his finger to the brim of his hat. "Carter."

"See you around, Chief."

Alain turned his blue gaze back to hers and she realized how wrong she'd been to think he was unmoved. His eyes were storm-cloud dark and the furrow between his brows looked carved into his skin. She wondered if anyone else felt the earth move under their feet the way she did when he said, "Sophie, I'll see you later."

ALAIN CLIMBED into the Explorer. The calendar might still say it was winter, but as far as he was concerned, it sure felt like spring. Maybe that was why he was so restless and at loose ends. Or it could be because Sophie had said she was going back to Houston in less than two weeks' time, and he wasn't ready for that to happen. He took a slow turn around the square. The talk he planned to have with her would have to wait a little while longer. He had a patrol to run, and an important errand to accomplish.

He pulled into a parking space in front of the Flower Basket. He needed to pick up the red roses he'd ordered for his mom and *Mamère* Yvonne for Valentine's Day before he forgot them and spoiled the effect by producing them a day late. He debated adding another rose to his order for Sophie but decided against it. If he got her anything it shouldn't be the same thing he'd chosen for his mother and grandmother. Besides, they weren't at that stage in their relationship yet. Hell, he couldn't truthfully say they had a relationship—yet.

Fifteen minutes later he was back on the road, two scarlet roses with sprigs of baby's breath and some kind of fern wrapped in green tissue paper on the seat beside him. Mission accomplished, he radioed the dispatcher that he was heading out along the River Road to make a loop past the Gator Trap and the B&B.

As usual, there wasn't much traffic on the road that skirted this portion of the Bayou Teche. In his five-mile swing through the countryside he met up with half a dozen farmers in pickups on their way to town, two beer delivery trucks and a FedEx van, and an adventurous tourist or two. Pretty easy to spot, what with their out-of-state license plates and pricey foreign cars. Still, snowbirds venturing off the well-marked Evangeline Trail this early in the season was a good sign.

Maybe the town Web site Estelle and Willis's son-in-law, over at the Chamber of Commerce, had set up was starting to draw some hits? Get the town noticed, put Indigo and the Valois Opera House on the path to fame and fortune as a tourist destination. At the moment, however, he was more worried about the upcoming Cajun Music Festival. He hoped the town council gave him the go-ahead—and the funds—to hire more part-time officers to beef up his force before thousands of music lovers descended on the town.

He slowed as he neared the turnoff to La Petite Maison, admiring the old house and the view of the bayou as he drove down the winding lane. He pulled into the graveled parking area at the side of the house, giving it the once-over as he backed into a turn. Sophie's car wasn't there, just a Volvo with Texas plates and a minivan with a Baton Rouge dealership sticker on the back panel. Two nondescript sedans appeared to be rentals. Carter had a full house for Valentine's weekend. Good for him.

He headed back into town. Sophie had probably passed him when he had pulled into the parking area at the public access to ask Deke Slayter how the catfish were biting. Back in town he cruised down Jefferson, keeping his eyes peeled for kids and stray dogs. There weren't too many stray dogs, but there were kids everywhere. Starting tomorrow, school was out for the rest of the week. Some kind of teacher's convention, or something down in Baton Rogue.

It was the weekend Casey Jo had wanted to take the kids to Disney World, but he hadn't heard anything from her in over a week so he was hoping she'd changed her mind. He could hope and pray and light candles to the Virgin that she'd stay away, but he wouldn't be a bit surprised if she did turn up.

He pulled to the curb in front of the opera house and looked in the front window of Past Perfect. Sophie's car was in its parking place but the store was closed up. Movement in the distance caught his attention and he saw her walking across the square from the direction of Maude's house. She was wearing the same sky-blue blouse she'd had on when he'd seen her earlier at the diner, but now he was treated to the sight of her swingy, dark-blue, calf-length skirt clinging to her legs and rounded hips in all the right places. He climbed out of the SUV and leaned one hip against the hood, watching her from behind the mirrored lenses of his sunglasses. Lord help him, she was a good-looking woman and he wanted her to be his.

"Alain," she said as she crossed the street and walked up to him. "I didn't think I'd see you again so soon."

"Quiet afternoon." He fell into step beside her as she climbed the low steps of the opera house.

"Beautiful afternoon," she amended. "I went for a walk after lunch and ended up at Maude's. Now that I've got the store under control, it's time I decided what to do with her house." She pushed her hand into the pocket of her skirt, drawing his eye to the enticing V at the top of her legs. He jerked his gaze back to eye level as she inserted the key into the deadbolt.

"Have any ideas?" he asked, holding open the door so she could precede him into the building.

"Nothing specific." She took off the white sweater she'd worn draped over her shoulders and hung it on a hook behind the counter. "I have to go through everything first. Decide what to keep, what to sell, what to give away. Then I'll talk to a Realtor. Maybe I'll rent it out for a year or so. Maybe I'll put a for sale sign on it right away. I've had one or two people tell me they might be interested in it."

Suddenly he knew he was one of those people. Not for him and the kids. It was too small. But for his mother. She'd always liked Maude's house. A doll's house she'd called it. She could be comfortable there. And what about her big old house on Lafayette Street? He could buy it from her. It was a good house for raising a family. He'd been happy growing up in it. His kids were happy living there. Would Sophie be happy there, too?

Lord, was he that far gone already? An hour ago he hadn't felt he could buy her a single damned rose for Valentine's Day, and now he was thinking about buying her a house? What about his vow not to get involved again until the kids were grown and on their own? It seemed he didn't have any qualms about breaking that one, either.

"Alain? Are you going to stand there letting in flies all afternoon?"

"What?" It was the teasing lilt in her voice that brought him back from his thoughts.

"Come inside and close the door. You're letting in

flies and dust. Do you know how long it takes to dust this place? Do you want to learn?"

"All right. All right. I get the point." He turned and shut the door very carefully and very quietly. *He was in love with her*. That's all there was to it. He could sidestep, split hairs; tell himself it was only lust, psychic residue, unfinished business, not *love,* but he'd be lying, and deep down inside he knew it. He loved her. Had always loved her in some form or another, and it wasn't going to go away.

But if he didn't make his move soon, she damned well might.

CHAPTER ELEVEN

"SOPHIE we have to talk."

She turned her head. He was standing with his feet planted wide, his hands folded across his waist. Her heart rate kicked up a notch or two. Lord, what was it about a man in a uniform? Or was it just this particular man in a uniform that made her want to stare at him all day and lie with him all night? She didn't even have to think about that one. It was the man who fascinated her, not what he wore.

"Yes, Alain?" What did he want to talk to her about? Did he want to ask her out for Valentine's Day? A date? She wouldn't object. Maybe he would kiss her again. She wouldn't object to that, either. She'd been thinking about his kisses for the last two days. And about more than kisses ever since the fireworks display was brought up at the meeting. The first time she'd made love with Alain had been after the Fourth of July fireworks that long-ago summer. She would never forget it. She wanted to make love like that again, in the backseat of his car, all heat and light and fiery passion.

She wanted to make love with Alain again—soon. But not in the middle of the showroom. "Come on back.

I have some more shuffling to do. The appraiser suggested I send the fainting couch and one or two other pieces to a dealer in New Orleans. She thinks I can double the asking price if I do that and Hugh's niece agrees." The woman had also suggested she send the Delacroix fiddle but she'd told her no. Not until she was certain Alain really didn't want it. She would have told him that, but she didn't think he'd come to talk about inventory.

She stepped into the auditorium and walked to the foot of the stairway leading to the private box. Once there, she needed something to do with her hands. She picked up one of the funny little overpriced stuffed animals that so intrigued Dana. "I'm afraid I've misplaced one of these toys your grandmother's cousin makes. You know, the one in Canada?"

"I've never met any of my Canadian cousins," he said. "And I don't know anything about one that makes stuffed animals. But then my mother has over two dozen first cousins alone. I can't even remember all their names, let alone the seconds and thirds up in Canada."

"Evidently this cousin makes these stuffed animals, ships them down and Maude sells…sold them for her. I guess she has a following here in Indigo." Sophie looked at the poor lopsided little frog, wondering, as she always did when she stopped to think about it, who would pay eighty dollars for such a misshapen creature?

"Dana has about a hundred stuffed animals, but Mom and *Mamère* Yvonne never mentioned anything about some of them being made by relatives in Canada."

"They're awfully pricey for children's toys. There's a bear in this batch that has a price tag of four hundred and seventy-five dollars."

"A stuffed bear?" That figure caught his attention. "You're right. That's way too pricey. Especially to let Dana play with." He had moved to stand beside her. She didn't turn around, but she could feel the heat of his body on her arm and shoulders, and it warmed parts of her that she'd ignored for years.

She steadied herself before she spoke again. "Your mom said it was probably a misprint on the label. She said she'd try and notify the people who ordered them. I've decided to put them out on display anyway. There aren't any names on the tags, no invoice with the shipment, so I have no way of knowing who they were meant to be for. Maybe people will see them in the window and contact me."

"That sounds reasonable," he said, then seemed to sense her agitation. "What's wrong?" he asked.

"What? Nothing." She picked up one or two animals, searching for the bear. "That's odd," she said, glad to have found a reason for her distraction that didn't involve sex. "I can't seem to find it. The teddy bear. It's not here."

He reached out and covered her hand with his. "We'll look for it later," he said in that smoky tone of voice that sent her insides quivering with want and need.

She dropped the frog among its companions. "Later," she agreed. "He probably fell out of the box when we were shifting everything around. He'll turn up under a seat or something. I'll give Guy and his buddies a couple of flashlights and send them bear-hunting the next time they show up."

"Good idea." He gave her arm a gentle tug, turning her to face him. "Sophie we need to talk about us."

She wasn't going to play coy. Him. Them. *Us.* It was all she thought about—at least in the dark, quiet hours of the night when she should have been asleep. "I don't know what you want to hear," she said truthfully.

"Did you mean what you said at the diner? That you're going back to Houston?"

"I want to see my grandparents. And there's my job and the expense. Luc's giving me a great rate at the B&B but I can't afford to stay there much longer. Especially now that he's starting to bring in real customers."

"Don't go back to Houston," he urged her, his voice smoky and rough. "Stay here. Give us a chance."

"A chance for what, Alain?" Her head was spinning and she realized she was holding her breath. She let it out, pulled air back into her lungs.

"This, for one thing." He bent his head to kiss her as he had in the cupola. But this time it was no gentle exploration. It was a taking, a claiming. He pulled her tight against him and she let herself go willingly. He was strong and hard and fitted her body in all the right places, just as she remembered. He increased the pressure of his mouth against hers, urging her to open to him. She did, welcomed him as their tongues mimicked a more intimate joining.

When the kiss was over she clung to him, too dazed to pull away. This was right. It was good. She had always liked the way he kissed but she had forgotten the full effect he had on her. Her knees were weak; her ears rang. She wanted to hold him so tight she sank into him and they became one. *Just as it had always been,* she admitted deep in her heart. *Just as it would always be.*

He stroked her hair with his big hand, held her face against his shirt. He smelled of soap and fabric softener—and Alain. "Don't go," he repeated, and she heard his voice shake. "Stay here. With me."

She wanted to. Oh, how she wanted to. But she was no longer a starry-eyed teenager, or a bereft young woman betrayed by the man she had unwisely chosen to take his place in her heart. She was an adult, with obligations and commitments. "It's not that easy, Alain. Not anymore."

"Sophie, I—"

A shaft of panic arrowed through her. She lifted her head, put her fingers to his lips. "Don't go too fast for me, Alain, please."

He brushed his fingers across her cheek, searched her face with his deep-blue eyes. He sighed. "Promise me you'll come back. Soon. So we can talk. Work out a plan."

"What kind of plan?"

"For our happily ever after."

"Oh, Alain." Her thoughts were an equal mix of pleasure and pain. She had wanted him, at some level, for so long but was it too late now? Were their lives on divergent paths, impossible to bring together?

"I know I shouldn't say this here and now, but I'm going to before I lose my nerve. We've sidestepped what's between us for too long. Sophie, I—" Somewhere in the back of her mind she heard the front door open and close, voices echo through the showroom. One a child's, Dana, laughing and excited. The other, hauntingly familiar, was a voice Sophie had hoped never to hear again.

Alain heard them, too. He stopped in midsentence, his eyes going bleak, his face hardening. Sophie's heart was still beating fast, but no longer from passion and anticipation, but with dread.

A figure appeared in the doorway and a mocking voice drawled, "I think I walked in on this scene once before."

Sophie took an instinctive step backward, hating herself for the spurt of guilt that rushed through her veins and sent color rising in her cheeks. How could the same embarrassing scene play itself out twice in her life? She felt as if she were one of those poor creatures who were struck by lightning a second time, even though the odds were millions to one against that happening. Alain held on to her hand, but when she tugged to be free he let her go, his mouth thinning to a straight line.

"Casey Jo, what are you doing here?"

"I was looking for our son. Your mother thought Guy might be here, but I can see she was mistaken about which one of you I'd find." Casey Jo's dark-rimmed, long-lashed eyes, as cold as green glass, flicked from Alain's stony face to Sophie's flushed one. "Ain't this just déjà vu all over again?"

She was still as pretty as Sophie remembered, but there was a hardness to her beauty now. Her hair was streaked with blond, but dark roots showed here and there. Her cheeks were surgically sculpted; her breasts enhanced and prominently displayed beneath a clinging black sweater and skin-tight capris. She was wearing strappy black, high-heeled sandals and long, swingy silver ear hoops, and she looked as out of place in Past Perfect as she could possibly be.

"Guy is at his driver's ed class. What are you doing here in Indigo?"

Her head came up. "You know perfectly well why I'm here. I came to take my babies to Disney World like I promised."

"We're going to leave first thing in the morning." Dana was almost dancing with excitement. "I wanted to pack my suitcase right away but Grandma said no. We had to come and talk to you first."

"Your mother wasn't going to let me take Dana out of the house. Did you put her up to that, Alain?"

"No, Casey Jo," he said, and his voice sounded weary, as though they had gone over this same ground countless times before.

"Well, you'd better not. I've never fought you for custody, but that doesn't mean I might not change my mind if you push me too far." Once more she let her gem-hard eyes flicker toward Sophie.

Dana was hanging on her mother's hand, looking up into her face. She switched her gaze to Alain, her eyes, so like Casey Jo's, pleading. "I want to go to Disney World, Daddy. I haven't got to see Momma for so long. We're going to have so much fun. She promised. Please."

"I don't know, baby," Alain said.

Dana didn't hear him; she had switched her attention to Sophie. "We're going to have breakfast with the princesses in the castle and everything—Momma promised." She repeated the words like a talisman, a magic spell that would make her dearest wish come true.

Sophie forced a smile. "That's nice, Dana." Her heart went out to the little girl, caught between a father she adored and relied on, and a mother who came and went in her life, but whom she also obviously loved and wanted to be with.

"I thought we'd settled this, Casey Jo," Alain said.

"I don't remember any such a thing," his ex-wife retorted with a toss of her dangling earrings. "Dana wants to go and I don't see why I shouldn't take her. If we start this afternoon we'll have two whole days at the park."

"It's a seven-hundred-mile drive." Sophie could see Alain was trying hard to hang on to his patience for Dana's sake. She was looking from one parent to another, the excitement in her green eyes fading into anxiety with each clipped exchange of words.

"So what? My car's in good shape."

The radio on Alain's belt crackled into life. "Chief Boudreaux, come in please."

"I'm here, Billy Paul."

"Frank Gillette says there's a gator come up in his yard and it's a big one. He called the sheriff's department, but they said they can't get anyone out there for another hour or two. He's afraid it might go after his dogs."

Alain pulled the radio off his belt clip and toggled the receiver. "I'll head out that way, but I doubt the gator's going to go after Frank's dogs. It's too cold. He's probably just sunning himself and he'll crawl back into the swamp in another hour or two."

"I tried telling Frank that," came the reply. "But he's worried about his darned old coon dogs. You know he thinks the world of those Catahoulas of his."

"I'll head on out that way, Frank. Call the sheriff and see if you can't hurry his guys up a little. Boudreaux out."

"An alligator! Daddy, can I ride with you and see it?" Dana was momentarily diverted from the subject of the disputed trip to Disney World.

"No, honey. I'm on duty. I can't take you with me." Dana's lower lip jutted out. Disappointment was written all over her elfin face. "Take her home, Casey Jo. We'll discuss the trip when I get there."

For a moment Sophie thought Alain's ex-wife was going to continue the argument, but she didn't. She smiled, a cat-in-the-cream kind of smile. "Come on, Dana, honey. Let's go pick up Grandma Marie and we'll all go get some ice cream. How does that sound?"

Dana began to jump up and down. "I love ice cream. I want chocolate chip with whipped cream and sprinkles on top."

"Casey Jo." There was nothing but steel in Alain's voice. "Take Dana straight back to my mother's when you're finished having ice cream."

"I'll take her back when we're finished visitin' with my mother," she shot back.

"Don't do anything foolish, Casey Jo," he warned.

She batted her improbably long lashes and gave him another smile, this one full of acid and animosity. "I wouldn't think of it, Alain."

They watched Casey Jo and Dana depart in silence.

"Damn. I'd hoped she'd decided not to push this Florida trip. But that's Casey Jo for you, always showing up to make life more complicated. I should have known better." He turned to face her. "I'm sorry, Sophie. I don't know what else to say about the way Casey Jo behaves."

"It's not your responsibility how she behaves. But maybe it was a good thing it happened. We were going a little too fast back down a path that landed us against a brick wall a couple of other times."

"Sophie." Again the radio on his belt crackled. Alain muttered a curse.

"Chief, you on your way out to Frank's place yet?" Billy Paul asked without preamble.

"I'm leaving right now."

"Well good. He just called back and says the gator made a charge at his dogs. I told him to shut them up in his barn but he says he don't want the darned thing coming after him, too."

"Unlock the weapons case. Break out a shotgun. I'll swing by and pick it up on my way out of town. Boudreaux out."

"I have to go, Sophie." He lifted his hand but she took a step back before he could take her in his arms. She wasn't ready for another mind-shattering kiss. She had too much to think about to have her thoughts clouded even more by passion and need. Alain's life was a complicated one. Was she ready to take on the responsibilities of being stepmother to his children if she uprooted herself and relocated to Indigo? Was she ready to have Casey Jo popping up whenever she felt like it to disrupt all their lives? "Go. Chase off the gator, then see to Dana and Guy."

"I'll be back," he promised. He didn't touch her, but she could feel the brush of his fingers across her cheek as surely as if he had.

He would be back, she didn't doubt his word.

But would she be waiting for him?

CHAPTER TWELVE

SOPHIE SPENT a restless night in her cozy suite tucked under the eaves. She was up early, foregoing the enticing smells of breakfast coming from the kitchen of La Petite Maison—except for a cup of Luc's excellent French-pressed coffee. Instead she headed into Indigo even before the sun had burned away the mist clinging to the surface of the bayou.

She didn't know why she was in such a hurry to return to Past Perfect. She would be better off spending the day in her comfortable, quiet room, perhaps sitting out on her little balcony, contemplating what she should do next.

Pack her bags and leave would be the most expedient choice.

But she'd done that twice before when Alain Boudreaux was concerned, and it wasn't an option this time. She was tired of trailing loose ends through her life.

But instead of driving to the store, she found herself pulling up in front of Maude's little house. The narrow, tree-lined street was quiet. Most of Maude's former neighbors were older couples, empty-nesters and retirees, although there were one or two young families fixing up larger houses down the street, Sophie had noticed. Indigo might be a very small town, but it was in no sense fading away. The population was stable and even growing, if slowly. She got out and walked up to the front porch, key in hand. She no longer felt overwhelmed by grief for her godmother when she opened the door. Instead she felt a sense of peace, that tantalizing, elusive sense of belonging that was so absent from her life in Houston. Maybe that was why she had come here today, to soak in that feeling, to let it seep into her pores and her mind and help guide her thoughts to a decision about her future and Alain.

It was a nice house; she'd always thought so. She'd like to keep it, but it wasn't big enough for a family. Alain was a package deal. He came with Dana and Guy in tow. That's what she would inherit if she let herself fall the rest of the way in love with him. A ready-made family. And an interfering ex-wife. Was she ready to accept that responsibility, too? Her head swam with all the decisions that faced her. Career. Marriage. Family.

She shook her head to clear the confusion as she unlocked the door. All this internal upheaval after only a couple of kisses. Would she have any mental faculties left after they made love? She doubted it. Was that why she'd chosen to stay at the B&B, despite the expense, instead of moving in here? Because she didn't trust herself alone with Alain with not one but two empty bedrooms only steps away? What would it be like to make love with him after so many years? She'd already asked herself that question, and answered it. She smiled; she couldn't help herself. It would be wonderful. No doubt about that.

So mind-bogglingly wonderful she probably wouldn't be able to make rational judgments afterward. So she needed to consider her options now.

"Hi, Sophie." She turned her head to see Dana standing out on the sidewalk. She was dressed in jeans and running shoes and a long-sleeved green sweater made from some sparkly material that matched her eyes. Over that she wore her red Winnie the Pooh raincoat with a matching hat, even though the sun was shining. She was dragging a wheeled suitcase along behind her. It was pink, with a trio of Disney princesses printed on the front. The child was a walking rainbow, and to Sophie, at least, she looked adorable.

"Hi, Dana, what are you doing out and about so early this morning?" Indigo wasn't Houston but it seemed very early for a seven-year-old to be out on her own, even here.

"I'm going to my grandma Marie's. My mommy is staying there. She and my daddy don't live together anymore, you know."

"I know." Sophie turned away from the door. She sat down on the top porch step and patted the seat beside her. It didn't take an expert on child behavior to figure out why Dana was dressed for a change in the weather and towing her suitcase. She was running away from Alain to be with her mother. "Come join me."

Dana looked over her shoulder. Her forehead crinkled into a frown. "I'm not supposed to stop and talk to people when I walk from Grandma Cecily's to Grandma Marie's. I'm supposed to go straight there." She pointed on down the street to the elderly duplex where Marie Lesatz lived.

"I won't keep you very long." Had Dana really run away or did she have Cecily Boudreaux's permission to go to her mother? Sophie decided she should find out. She patted the seat beside her again. "You can stay just for a minute, can't you?"

"Okay. But only one minute." Dana parked her little suitcase by the step and sat down beside Sophie. "My mommy's waiting for me."

"Oh, then she knows you're on your way," Sophie probed gently.

Dana looked down at the toes of her scuffed runners. "Well, no. Grandma Marie works at night. She's still asleep so I didn't want to call and wake her up."

"What about Grandma Cecily? Does she know where you're going?"

"She's at the hospital." Dana started picking at a worn spot on her jeans. "Guy's still asleep 'cause there's no school. And *Mamère* Yvonne's taking a nap on the couch. Her medicine makes her sleepy after she takes it in the morning. Everyone's asleep but me." She looked up. Her beguiling smile twisted Sophie's heart. "And my daddy. He's at work taking care of the whole town."

"I know." So she *was* running away. Sophie wondered if she should make some kind of excuse to go inside and use her cell to call Alain? If she did that, Dana would never trust her again, and she didn't want that. But if she did nothing and Casey Jo left town with the little girl, Alain would never trust her again, either.

She decided to stall for time. "What's in your bag?"

The smile faded. Dana scooted away from Sophie. "Just stuff."

"Okay." Sophie was running out of small talk. She decided to stop tiptoeing around the issue. "Dana, does your daddy know you're going to visit your mama?"

Dana fixed her green eyes on the top button of Sophie's sweater, not on her face. "I'm allowed." Her little chin jutted out. "I'm allowed to go to Grandma Marie's."

"I think we should call your father and make sure," Sophie said, knowing she had to act.

"No!" Dana jumped off the step and grabbed her suitcase so violently it tipped over sideways.

Sophie stood up and descended the steps to help her right it. "Your grandma Yvonne will be worried when she wakes up from her nap and finds you gone."

"I can go to Grandma Marie's by myself. I can."

From the corner of her eye Sophie saw a bicycle turn onto the street from Lafayette. She recognized Guy and felt relieved that she wouldn't have to be the one to rat Dana out.

From the opposite direction a ten-year-old Taurus pulled up to the curb and Casey Jo jumped out. She was wearing biker shorts and a faded Saints T-shirt and her hair was pulled up in a knot on top of her head. She wasn't wearing makeup, and while she was still very pretty, she looked her age. "Dana, what are you doing here?"

"She took off without telling us," Guy answered for her as he skidded up on his bike. "*Mamère* Yvonne woke up and found her gone and sent me after her."

"She called us, too," Casey Jo said. Her green eyes were fixed on her son's face, as though she were drinking in his features. "You didn't stop by to see me last night like you said you would."

Guy dropped the bike in the grass and went over to pick up his sister's suitcase and set it back on its wheels on the sidewalk. "I said I *might* come over. I was busy. Sorry," he added grudgingly as he straightened to face her.

She reached out a hand to touch his cheek. "You're so tall," she said, tilting her head back a little to meet his eyes. "You didn't look that tall in the pictures Grandma Marie sent me."

"Yeah, well, if you'd show up here more than every year or so, it wouldn't be such a shock when you see me up close and personal, would it?"

"Watch your mouth," Casey Jo snapped, then made as if to pull him into her arms, her eyes filled with easy tears. "I'm sorry, baby. I shouldn't have said that. I'm really sorry."

Guy evaded her embrace. "Yeah," he said, wrapping his hands around Dana's shoulders. "That's what you always say."

"I'm busy, Guy. I have to earn a living. You'd see that if you ever came to visit me."

"Trying out for *American Idol* isn't making a living. C'mon, Dana, we're going home."

"No," Dana whimpered. "I miss Mommy. I want to go with her to Disney World."

"Come to Mama, darlin'."

"Stay here." Guy tightened his hands on Dana's shoulders to hold her still and she started to cry.

"Ouch, you're hurting me," she sniffled, squirming to be set loose.

Casey Jo wiggled her fingers. "Baby, come here."

"You're not taking her anywhere," Guy said, but he let Dana go. "I called Dad. He's on his way."

Sophie didn't know what to say or do next. She felt like an interloper, a bystander caught in the eye of an emotional hurricane. Uncomfortable as she was, she stood her ground. Her heart ached for Guy and Dana and she didn't intend to walk away and leave them alone with Casey Jo until Alain arrived.

"Why'd you do that, Guy?" Casey Jo said as she knelt and gathered Dana into her arms. "We could have sorted this all out at Grandma's. Now we'll have to air our dirty linen in front of her." She flicked a damning glance at Sophie.

"Considering you're standing on my property, I should be the one asking you to leave," Sophie replied. Casey Jo Lesatz had caused her to cut and run once. It wasn't going to happen again.

"My mama said old Maude Picard dropped over dead and left you everything." She gave the little house a dismissive once-over before turning her gaze back to Sophie. "Some people just naturally fall into the honeypot, don't they?"

Sophie remained silent, determined not to be goaded.

Alain's SUV pulled up behind Casey Jo's run-down compact and he ate up the distance from the curb to the porch in half a dozen strides. "What's going on?" he asked, taking in the four of them with a single sweep of his eyes.

"Dana snuck out of the house," Guy said before anyone else could speak. "*Mamère* Yvonne dozed off, and when she woke up, Dana was gone. We figured she was walking to Grandma Marie's and we were right. Here she is."

"Mama figured the same thing and I came lookin' for her the minute your grandmama called," Casey Jo inserted. She stood up, holding Dana tight against her. "She wants to go to Florida with me and I'm taking her."

"I thought we thrashed this all out last night," Alain said, his tone patient but hard-edged. "It's seven hundred miles to Orlando. That's too long a trip to make in three days."

"We'll have four days if you stop jawing at me and let us get on the road," Casey Jo shot back.

"How do we know you're even planning on coming back?" Guy interrupted. "For all we know, you'll just keep Dana with you."

"Why, I'd never do that," she said bitterly. "Your father would probably have me hauled off to jail if I did."

"Daddy wouldn't do that," Dana whimpered, throwing her arms around her mother's waist. "Would you, Daddy?" She'd grown very quiet after Alain arrived, the excitement in her animated little face replaced with anxiety. "We'll come back, won't we? I get to clean the blackboards next week. And it's my turn to take our class hamster home for the weekend."

"Sure, sweet baby. Mama will bring you back here on Sunday. I promise." For the first time Sophie felt sorry for Casey Jo as she saw the other woman absorb the sting of Dana's words. She might be far from the best mother in the world, but no woman should have to hear her children tell her they didn't want to stay with her.

Alain must have seen the hurt the innocent statement inflicted because his voice softened when he spoke again. He hunkered down in front of the little girl. "Dana, you won't get to stay at Disney World very long. Florida is very far away. You know you get carsick when you have to ride a long time. It's not too late to tell Mama you would rather go some other time."

Dana shook her head, her eyes filling with disappointed tears. "I won't get carsick. I want to go with Mama. Please. We're going to have so much fun. She promised." All the pent-up anticipation of a seven-year-old poured into her words and her voice.

"She always promises," Guy said, shoving his hands into the pockets of his jeans. "You know that."

"We'll have fun," Dana insisted. "Daddy, please."

Alain remained balanced on the balls of his feet, his arms wrapped around his daughter. Sophie ached for him. For the decision he faced. Around them she heard the neighborhood come to life. Dogs barked, doors slammed and car engines rumbled as people went off to work and morning errands, but Alain remained silent.

Finally he lifted his head and set Dana away from him. He rose to his feet and turned his full attention to his ex-wife. "Have her back here by 7:00 p.m. Sunday or I'll come after you myself. And yes, I will have you arrested. I'll do it in the blink of an eye. Do you understand?"

Casey Jo's eyes glittered like green glass but she didn't contradict him. "I'll have her back on time." She turned to Guy, the angry line of her mouth transforming into a dazzling smile as she held out her hand. "Come with us, Guy. Give us a chance to get to know one another again."

Guy threw up his hands in disgust. "No! I'm not going with you. And I can't believe Dad's letting Dana go, either. You'll just mess it up like you always do and she'll come home crying. I hate you both." He turned on his heel and jumped on his bike.

"Well, thanks for that, Alain," Casey Jo said bitterly, as she watched Guy ride away. "I could have talked him around if you hadn't put up such a damned fuss over this whole thing."

Alain picked up Dana's little pink suitcase and walked toward the car. "No, you couldn't, Casey Jo. He's not seven. He's fifteen and you can't talk your way around him anymore. And if you screw up this visit with Dana, you won't be able to paper over the cracks with her as easily as in the past, either. Remember that." He tossed the suitcase into the backseat, leaned down and buckled Dana into her seatbelt. He gave her a kiss and shut the door. Resting both hands on the top of the car, he stared at Casey Jo over the roof of the vehicle and the steel in his voice sent shivers up and down Sophie's spine. "Don't blow it, Casey Jo, or you'll never be alone with her again."

WATCHING Casey Jo drive away with Dana was the hardest thing Alain had ever done. God, what if she didn't come back on Sunday? He'd talked a big game but he got Amber Alerts at the station every day for children who were abducted by family members, and some of them were never seen again. Guy would never forgive him if that happened to Dana. And he would never forgive himself.

"Come on inside. I'll make you a cup of coffee."

He spun on his heel. Sophie was still standing at the foot of the porch steps. He wouldn't have blamed her if she'd gone inside, slammed the door in his face and locked it after the scene she'd just witnessed. But she didn't turn her back on him. She smiled and waited for him to respond. She looked like a breath of springtime in a yellow flowered skirt and white blouse. Her hair was a halo of golden curls that framed her face and caressed the rose petals in her cheeks.

"I could use something stronger than coffee." He didn't know what to do next. Go after Guy. Go after Casey Jo and tell her he'd changed his mind about letting her take Dana to Disney World. Or follow Sophie into Maude's little house. His feet started moving toward her before his conscious mind gave them the command.

"I thought cops weren't allowed to drink on duty."

"We aren't." He hesitated, wondering if he should take off after Guy instead.

"Come on in, Alain. Guy needs some time to settle down, and Casey Jo won't be leaving town for at least an hour. I imagine it takes her that long to put on her makeup. You've still got time to stop her if you feel that's what you have to do."

She'd read his mind. Alain felt a smile tug at the corners of his mouth despite the heaviness in his heart. Sophie was right about Casey Jo's face. It always took his ex-wife at least an hour of primping in front of a mirror to satisfy herself that she was ready to face the world each morning.

"How did you know that's what I was thinking?" he asked, mounting the steps.

Sophie looked at him over her shoulder as she preceded him down the hall to the kitchen. His footsteps rang hollowly on the hardwood floor. The house had taken on the empty feeling houses always got when there was no one living in them.

"Because that's exactly what I'd be asking myself if I was in your shoes."

"You believe I shouldn't have let Dana go with her mother, don't you?"

She didn't answer him right away. She pulled a small can of coffee out of the cupboard, opened it and sniffed the contents. "Still good." She ran water into the coffeemaker and spooned coffee into the basket. When the dark liquid began to run into the carafe, she turned and faced him, her hands braced on the counter on either side of her. "Do you believe Dana's at risk of being harmed in some way when she's with Casey Jo?"

"At risk of having her little heart broken, maybe," he said, searching inwardly for telltale signs of doubt. He met Sophie's questioning gaze head-on. "But she's not in any physical danger. Casey Jo's selfish and immature, but she's not a fool. She'll take care of Dana. I wouldn't have let her go otherwise."

Sophie took a mug from the cupboard, rinsed it in the sink and waited until enough coffee had filled the carafe. She poured a cup for Alain and handed it to him.

"But you do have fears she might not bring her back. Am I mistaken there?"

"I think about that happening every time the woman comes to town. I think most single parents do from time to time."

"Why did you let her go with her mother, then?"

He wrapped his hand around the thick mug, and took a sip of strong, hot coffee before he replied. He was too restless to sit. So was Sophie, evidently. She remained standing, her back to the counter while he considered his answer. "I guess I let her go because I'm tired of always being the bad guy. And Casey Jo isn't some kind of monster. She's just thoughtless and immature. And maybe, deep down, I hoped she would give Dana the time of her life so she'd have some good memories to fall back on when the next disappointment comes. Because there will be more disappointments. Casey Jo's not ever going to grow up."

"You really believe that?"

He studied the coffee that remained in his mug. "I haven't seen much improvement in the five years we've been apart. So, no, I'm not too hopeful."

"Now you've got to convince Guy you made the right decision."

He set the half-empty mug on the table. "That's not going to be easy. He doesn't have any of those happy memories to fall back on himself."

CHAPTER THIRTEEN

SOPHIE LOOKED OUT the window of Past Perfect at the pouring rain. The clouds had rolled in on Thursday afternoon and by midnight she had heard the drumbeat of raindrops on the roof of La Petite Maison. Now it was Friday afternoon and it was still raining. And not just in Indigo. The low-pressure system extended all across the Gulf States and into Florida. It was beginning to look like this would be the wettest winter in southwest Louisiana in almost a century.

Dana would need her bright red Winnie the Pooh raincoat at Disney World because it was going to rain in Orlando, too. Sophie had checked the weather maps on her laptop when she got up that morning.

"Anything else you want me to do before I leave, Miss Sophie?" Guy asked. She hadn't met a male yet, old or young, in Indigo who didn't address her in that charmingly old-fashioned manner. She was beginning to not only get used to it, but enjoy it.

"I think that's all for today, Guy. Thanks for the help." He was wearing a shiny black windbreaker over an Indigo High sweatshirt and would probably be soaked by the time he got home. She wondered if she should offer him a ride but decided against it. He played football in the rain; he could walk the four blocks to his grandmother's house in the same conditions.

Sophie tucked the lopsided frog into a corner of the armoire shelf where she'd arranged the other stuffed animals and stepped back to admire her handiwork. "What do you think, Guy?" she asked, spreading her hands. "I gather there's a group of people who collect them. But I haven't been able to find any documentation of who these were ordered for so I'm putting them out here. Dana told me my godmother sometimes displayed them here. Maybe I can find their intended owners this way."

"Looks good," he said. "Sorry I couldn't find the bear."

"That's okay. It will turn up." But she was beginning to wonder. They'd swept out all the dust bunnies from under the seats in the auditorium, upended drawers and shone flashlights in all the dark corners, but the bear hadn't turned up. Was it possible someone had stolen the toy? She thought that unlikely; there had been no signs of a break-in, and no customers since her godmother died, so shoplifting seemed unlikely. But still, the price had been so ridiculously high.

She really ought to call Alain's mother and inform her of the loss. She was Sophie's only real contact with the woman who had made the animals.

"If that's all, I'll be taking off," Guy said.

"Have you heard from Dana?" she asked. She had resisted the temptation to quiz him so far, but now her resolve failed. She hadn't yet seen Alain that day and

she was anxious for news of Dana. Alain had told her
yesterday, when they crossed paths in the General
Store, that Casey Jo and Dana had spent the night
before near Tallahassee. He figured they would be in
Orlando by early afternoon. It was now a little after
four.

"Not today." Guy's dark, angled brows pulled
together in a frown just as Alain's did when he was
worried. She wanted a son with those same dark brows
and strong nose. Thoughts like that made her anxious
to return to Houston. She needed to step back and take
stock of her life before she did something she might
regret for the rest of her days.

"She's probably having too much fun," Sophie said,
knowing how lame the platitude sounded. She hoped
she was right, though. Hoped that Dana was, this very
moment, whirling around in a giant teacup, squealing
with delight.

"She was still supposed to call me. I gave her my old
phone so she'd have one of her own."

"Maybe she lost it. Or forgot to charge the battery.
She's only seven," Sophie reminded him gently.

"Yeah, maybe. Or maybe something's wrong." He
set his jaw and jammed his hands in the pockets of his
jeans. "My dad thinks Dana will be okay with her but
I'm not so sure." The deliberate omission of his
mother's name wasn't lost on Sophie.

She hesitated before asking any more questions. She
wasn't certain how far into his confidence Guy would
take her. Or how far she should try to probe. Did her
renewed love for Alain entitle her to counsel his son?

She decided to take it one question at a time, relying on her own good judgment to warn her when to back off. "Did anything like that ever happen when you were with your mother?"

He gave her a long, considering look, then nodded. "She took me to the mall one day when I was little. And when I got tired she set me down on a bench and left me there. For hours it seemed, while she went off looking for new shoes. I had to go to the bathroom really bad and I started to cry. Finally a security guy came over and asked me what was wrong. I was afraid to tell him. I was so dumb I thought I would get in trouble, not her. He was going to take me to the mall office and page her, except I thought it must be a jail. I really started to wail. You could hear me all over the mall. Just then, she came back."

"Did you tell your father about it?"

"No. She cried and cried and said she was sorry and that it would make Dad mad at both of us if I told him about it. For a long time I thought the whole thing *was* my fault. I don't want my sister feeling like that."

"I can understand why you wouldn't. I wish you'd tell your father what happened. It would make it easier for him to understand where you're coming from."

"I suppose," he admitted grudgingly.

"He might have changed his mind if he'd known she left you alone like that," she added gently. *So far, so good,* she thought. She hadn't said anything yet to send him stomping off into the rain.

"Yeah, I thought of that, too." He yanked up the zipper of his windbreaker. "But it's too late now. Look.

I gotta go. I'll be back in the morning with Antoine to hang the reopening banner." Amelia Prejean had agreed to start work on Monday. Sophie would plan some sort of back-in-business celebration for later, when the weather was better, but for now she just wanted to get the cash flow moving again. There were bills to be paid.

Guy pulled open the door of the opera house and the smell of rain swirled in on the wet air. Sophie had told herself she was only a sounding board for him, not a mentor, not a *parent*. But she couldn't stop herself from offering her opinion. "Guy," she called as he stepped outside. He looked back at her, pulling up the hood of his windbreaker. "Try not to worry too much about Dana. Remember, your dad has good instincts. He wouldn't have let her go with your mother otherwise."

He gave a curt nod, acknowledging her words, and loped off into the rain.

For a few days it had seemed as if spring wasn't too far away. But it had been an illusion. The wind was cold and wet as Alain got out of the Explorer and mounted the porch of Maude's little house. Lights were burning in the living-room window and in the kitchen.

He rang the bell, watching as Sophie's willowy figure came toward him, hips swaying gently, her silhouette frosted by the etched-glass door, just as his breath was frosted by the cold.

"Alain," she said, her smile warming him from the inside out. "Come in out of the rain."

"Thanks." He stepped directly into the fussy,

crowded living room. He lifted his head, sniffed appreciatively. The slightly musty, unlived-in smell was gone, replaced by...chocolate chip cookies.

Sophie's smile turned into a grin. "Don't get your hopes up. It's not cookies. It's a candle. I brought it over from the shop."

"Too bad. I could use a couple of warm chocolate chip cookies."

"That hard a day?" she asked, concern darkening her eyes. Was he just imagining it or was she holding herself aloof from him, withdrawing slightly? He couldn't blame her if she started having second thoughts about getting involved again, especially after Cascy Jo had barged back into their lives.

"I've had better. Three fender benders and two vandalism complaints out on the River Road. Probably the same kids spray-painting gang signs on outbuildings."

"Gang signs?" She looked incredulous. "Gangs in Indigo?"

"The kids pick up on the signs and the colors, stuff like that, but they don't have one damn inkling of what it truly signifies. I've got a good idea who it is. I'll talk to their parents tomorrow, see if we can work some kind of deal with the barn owners and keep them out of court." They weren't bad kids and there was no reason in his mind to hang a juvenile rap around their necks.

"In other words you've been out in the rain all day."

"Most of it," he agreed.

"I don't have any chocolate chip cookies but I do have oyster stew from the Blue Moon and a loaf of Loretta's fruit-and-spice bread that's a meal in itself. There's plenty. We can share."

"Thanks, I'd like that." More than like, he thought to himself. It was his idea of heaven. Sophie bustling about in the kitchen, handing him bowls and plates from the cupboard to set the table; the smell of coffee brewing as the rainy darkness pressing against the windows was kept at bay by the warmth of her voice and the brightness of her smile. "You've been spending a lot of time here the last couple of days."

She looked around the kitchen at the country blue-and-rose wallpaper and the brick-patterned linoleum that was at least twenty years out of date, the appliances that were a decade older than that, the shelves of knickknacks and salt-and-pepper shakers, and nodded. "I know I have. It's time for me to start going through Maude's things here. At first it made me too sad to think of, so I stayed away. Lately, though…" She shrugged and looked down at her plate, not meeting his eyes. "It's beginning to feel like home—" She broke off and then corrected herself. "I mean, it feels like Maude's home again, not just an empty house."

"I noticed that, too, when I came in. Maybe it was the candle."

She looked up and smiled. "And the soup. Sit down. Eat while it's hot." She was quiet a moment as he took off his jacket and laid it over the back of a chair.

"Look at you," she said, laughing. "You're out of uniform."

He glanced down at his jeans and dark-gray chamois shirt. "I do occasionally wear civvies."

"I was beginning to wonder," she said, still smiling. She motioned to a chair. "Sit." When he was seated she asked, "Have you heard from Dana today? I asked Guy earlier but he said no."

"Nothing," he said curtly.

"They're probably having too much fun to stop and phone home." Her smile remained in place but she couldn't mask the concern in her voice.

"It's raining there, too."

"I know."

"Guy's worried about Dana," she said, setting a bowl of steaming soup in front of him.

"I spoke to him a little while ago." Alain picked up his spoon. It was old-fashioned silver, heavy and ornate, made to fit a man's hand. "I know he has a lot of issues with his mother, but he's really got himself tied into a knot over this Disney trip." He looked across the table at Sophie as she sat down with her own bowl of soup. "It's not the first time I've allowed Casey Jo to have custody of Dana for a day or two. But it is the farthest away she's ever taken her. God help me, I hope I didn't make a mistake."

"So does Guy," Sophie said, buttering a slice of the fragrant spice bread before handing it to him. "Did he tell you why he's so worried about Casey Jo taking Dana this time?"

"Not really," Alain confessed. "I've got the feeling there's more to it than he's telling me, but he won't give me any details." She was looking down at her soup, spoon poised. "Sophie, did he tell you why he's so angry?"

She didn't answer him, or look up from her plate for a long moment. "Yes," she said, finally meeting his eyes, her blue-gray gaze troubled. "But I don't know if I should pass on what he said."

"You have to tell me, Sophie. What happened? Did Casey Jo hurt him?" She had never been abusive to the kid. Thoughtless and careless, yes. But she had never hurt them. Or had she? Alain's blood ran cold in his veins. "Did she hurt him, Sophie? I have to know."

"Not physically," Sophie said quickly, holding up her hand as though cautioning him to rein in his stampeding thoughts. "But she left him alone in a mall when he was very small. Long enough, evidently, to frighten him so badly he's never forgotten it. He's afraid something like that will happen to Dana, too."

Alain wanted to slam the spoon down on the table, or throw the soup across the room, anything to relieve the surge of anger and guilt that shot into his veins. "I never knew. He never told me." His mind raced back to the years he and Casey Jo had been together in New Orleans when Guy was very small. "I was working double shifts on the New Orleans PD then. I was gone a lot. If he remembers that one incident, there were probably others. How the hell could I have been so blind?"

"You weren't blind," Sophie said, reaching out to cover the fist he'd made around his spoon with her warm, comforting fingers. "You just said you were working double shifts. You were gone most of the time, trying to make a better life for your wife and child. You couldn't have known what she was doing with Guy every hour of the day."

"She was neglecting him even then and I should have recognized it. Damn. That makes me as bad a parent as she is."

"Don't be ridiculous," she said sharply. She withdrew her hand. "All right. Maybe you should have recognized the signs with Guy, and maybe not. Maybe it did only happen once. You need to ask him."

"That's not going to do me any good tonight."

"No, but it will in the future. Did you have any suspicion she was neglecting Dana?"

"No," he said flatly. "She didn't stick around long enough after Dana was born to neglect her. She was an accident, my sweet baby. Our final attempt at a reconciliation. It didn't last long enough for me even to suspect Casey Jo was pregnant. We never shared a bed again, even though it was another two years before she took off for good."

He rested his elbows on the table and covered his left fist with his right hand. He felt the chill as the warmth of her fingers faded from his skin. He looked at her, expecting to see the same loathing in her expression he was feeling for himself at the moment. Instead he saw compassion and something more underlying the blue of her eyes, like smoke swirling in the twilight sky. Something deeper, richer than empathy for his pain. Was it love, or only a reflection of what he felt for her?

"You haven't made any worse mistakes than a lot of other parents."

"I should have sat Guy down and made him tell me why he was so angry with Casey Jo a long time ago."

She leaned slightly forward, her hands flat on the

table top. "Granted, you should have talked to Guy, but that's no guarantee he would have told you what he told me."

"Why not?"

"Because he's fifteen and you're his father. He doesn't need any other reason than that. And you're both stubborn Boudreaux men." She smiled. "He's begun to realize he was wrong not to tell you about what happened. He's a smart kid. He understands now that his silence helped put his sister in the kind of situation he endured when he was small. He's as angry with himself as he is with you for allowing the visit in the first place."

Alain finished his soup in silence. What she said made a lot of sense. Guy was a proud kid. He took his role as Dana's big brother and protector seriously. He would be as mad at himself as he was with Alain. "I should be getting home," he said, getting up from the table. "Casey Jo might have called her mother, or mine. And I have to talk to Guy, work this out."

Sophie came around the table to him. "You'll let me know when you hear from Dana and Casey Jo?"

"Of course." He didn't like the faint hint of distance he heard in her voice, the feeling that she was pulling back from him. He wasn't going to wait any longer to tell her what was on his mind. He'd waited too long already. There was never going to be a perfect moment. He reached for her instead of his coat. For a moment he thought she would step away, but slowly her muscles relaxed and she slipped her arms around his waist, laid her head against his chest. "Sophie, there's something

I have to tell you, to ask you." His heart began to thud against his ribs. He supposed she could hear it.

She lifted her head to stare up at him. "Alain, I wish you wouldn't," she whispered. Sadness darkened her eyes to a foggy gray. "Not yet."

"You know what I'm going to say," he said, framing her face with his hands. "I love you, Sophie. Part of me has always loved you, even during all those years when I tried as hard as I could to put you completely out of my mind." Like the last red-gold ember of a dying fire buried in ash, the love he had felt for her for more than a dozen years had needed only a breath of air to stir it to life.

"I know," she said, tears shimmering on her lashes. "I've always felt that way about you, too. But that doesn't mean it will work between us now any better than it would when we were teenagers."

"Can't you give us a chance?" He laid his forehead against hers. "Sophie, will you—"

"No." She pressed her fingertips to his lips. "Don't say any more."

The words cut into his heart. "Sophie, I know I've got a lot of complications in my life right now. The kids—"

"The kids aren't the problem. They're wonderful kids. I'd be the happiest woman on earth if they were mine. And it's not Casey Jo that's the problem. At least, not all of it. It's me, Alain. You're a man who will need an extraordinary woman to handle all the complications in your life. I'm not sure I've got what it takes."

"You just admitted you could love me again."

"Sometimes that's not enough." She placed her hands on his chest, holding herself away from him. "My track record in marriage isn't any better than yours. I got burned badly. It almost destroyed me. I don't know if I want to make that kind of commitment again." She brushed her tears aside with the back of her hand. "I'm not going to cry," she said fiercely. "I'm trying to tell you what's in my heart. I'm not going to mess it up with tears. I've got a life and a career in Houston, Alain. I'm not sure I'm ready to give that up. And that's what promising myself to you would mean. Indigo's where you belong. Once upon a time I thought I could belong here, too. But that was a long time ago. Now I'm not so naive or so brave to think that love is all it takes."

"Don't you believe in second chances?" he asked, using all his willpower not to pull her back into his arms and never let her go.

She laid her fingers against his cheek. "I think that week seven years ago was our second chance." The sadness in her voice chilled him to the marrow.

"Then how about three time's a charm?" he said, using the pad of his thumb to wipe a stray teardrop from her cheek.

She shook her head. "Not three's the charm. It's three strikes and you're out. I'm going back to Houston, Alain. Monday morning. I don't know when I'll be back."

CHAPTER FOURTEEN

"NOTHING in that fridge is going to mutate into anything else while you're standing there with the door open."

"What?"

"I thought you told me Grandma Yvonne put righteous fear into you about standing in front of an open refrigerator door?"

Alain twisted his head to regard his son lounging against the kitchen door frame, then looked back at the contents of the refrigerator and blinked. How long had he been standing there staring into space? "Sorry. My mind was somewhere else." He grabbed a bottle of water and shut the door with a snap.

"Did Dana call while I was out?"

Alain twisted the cap off the bottle of overpriced water with more violence than necessary. "No."

"It's Saturday night. They've been gone since Thursday. How long are you going to wait?" Guy's tone wasn't combative enough to call him on, but he was coming close.

"I gave your mother until seven o'clock tomorrow evening to have her home." He sat down at the kitchen table and made a pretense of rolling back the cuffs of his faded plaid shirt. He took another swallow of water, waiting for Guy's next move.

His son snorted in disgust, but came to sit beside him at the kitchen table instead of turning on his heel and stomping out of the room. The kid hadn't exactly been avoiding him for the last couple of days, but he'd sure made himself scarce when Alain was around the house.

"I just tried Mom's cell again. It's turned off." So that was it. He *was* worrying about Dana. It was unusual for him to stick around the house on a Saturday evening. He was generally off with friends, watching videos, playing computer games, hanging out at the General Store to watch the girls watching the guys as they bought sodas and snacks and rented videos for sleep-overs.

He ran with a good bunch of kids, so Alain didn't worry too much about what they were up to, but he realized things were about to change. Guy would have a driver's license in another six months, and so would the other kids. They were going to want to start wandering farther afield than the General Store or one of their friends' rec rooms. They'd want to go to Lafayette to the movies or on fast-food binges. And there would be car dates with girls. *Lord, where had the time gone?*

"You should have made a stipulation about her checking in once in a while."

"Yeah, I guess I should have." He'd screwed up there big-time. Casey Jo had him right where she wanted him this weekend and she was enjoying being the one calling the shots. He could deal with her playing these little games, but not if they compromised Dana and Guy's welfare. "I won't make that mistake again," he said.

Guy traced a design on the table top with his cell. It was a picture phone, barely bigger than a matchbox, and it had cost plenty, but Guy had paid for it with his own money so Alain had let him buy it. The silence stretched out. Alain listened as the washer on the back porch whined into the spin cycle and a piece of loose change clattered away in the dryer. "I think you made a bigger mistake letting Dana go with her, at all," Guy replied with a shade less animosity in his voice. He didn't meet Alain's gaze, but kept his eyes on the twists and turns he was making with his phone.

Alain had wanted to broach the subject since Sophie had told him about her conversation with the boy, but Guy hadn't given him a chance. Now it was his son who had brought it up. He didn't want to let on just how much he knew. He wouldn't break Sophie's confidence. "Why do you say that, son?"

"She left me alone in the mall once when I was really little. She just plunked me down on a bench and took off. She was gone a long time. I was there so long a security guard thought I was lost. I was scared and hungry and I had to go to the bathroom so bad I thought I'd pee my pants. I cried and cried. Because I figured the guard would take me to jail for being alone." The words came out in a rush. Guy paused and took a breath, getting control of himself. "Little kids think of screwy things like that, y'know. And when she got back she told me never to tell you or you'd be really mad at me for causing a scene. Not at her for leaving me alone all that time."

"I'm sorry, Guy. I never knew that happened. I wish you'd told me about it before tonight."

The cell-phone design grew in complexity. "Yeah, I see that now. But all the time I was growing up, I figured you knew. When you're little and something like that happens, you think your mom and dad know everything in the world and you believe what they say." He shot Alain a quick glance. "But lately I...I talked to a friend about it and I realized you couldn't have known if no one told you."

"Did your mom leave you alone other times? Times when I wasn't home?"

Guy shrugged. "She might have. Never that long though or I'd remember. Funny, I never remember her hitting me, or even yelling at me a whole lot. Only leaving me that one day. It seemed like she was gone forever." He stopped working the elaborate design and flipped open the phone, still without meeting Alain's eyes. "I don't want that to happen to Dana. Especially in some place as big as Disney World."

"I don't want that, either." It was Alain's turn to trace designs on the table. He moved the water bottle around in ever-widening circles. "I've always done the best I could for both of you." A lump formed in his throat and he swallowed it down, but the residue made his voice rough around the edges. "You two are my whole life. You know that, don't you?"

Guy lifted his eyes from the tiny screen of his phone. His Adam's apple jumped up and down. "I know, Dad.

I was never afraid again after we moved to Indigo. I guess I knew by then that you'd be there to take care of me. Of both of us. That's why I went ballistic the other day. It always seemed like you were almost as smart as a superhero or something, and somehow you should have known about that day, too."

"I hate to tell you this, pal, but dads don't know everything."

Guy's lip curled into a half smile. "No kidding."

"I'm sorry that your mom scared you that way when you were so little and helpless, but since you don't remember any other incidents like that, it makes me feel a little better thinking it was a one-time thing. Your mom's not a bad person, Guy. She's just…"

"Sort of like a female Peter Pan." Guy clicked the phone shut and closed his palm around it. It disappeared and Alain realized his son's hands were almost the size of his own. "She's probably having more fun at Disney World than Dana is and that's why she hasn't called. Not because she's kidnapped Dana and run off with her to start a new life somewhere."

"That's what I believe." *Dear Lord, he hoped he was right.*

"Why did you have to marry her, Dad?"

Once more Alain was caught off guard. He'd expected arguments and recriminations, raised voices. Instead he was talking to an image of the man his son would soon become, not the boy he had been only a day or two before.

"She was pregnant with you." He wasn't going to lie and say he loved her. He owed Guy's new-found maturity that much honesty.

Color stained his cheeks but Guy didn't look away. "I can count. What I mean is, why did you think you had to marry her just because she was going to have a baby? Lots of guys wouldn't do that. One or two guys in school brag about it. Making babies but not having to marry the girl."

"I married her because it was the right thing to do, and I hoped we could learn to be happy with each other. We were probably too young, but I gave it my best shot."

"Did Mom?"

"If I told you she did the best she could, would you think better of her or worse?"

Guy's mouth twisted in a half smile. "That's one of the lady-or-the-tiger questions, isn't it?"

"I guess it is."

"I've finally figured out she's never gonna be a real mom to me or Dana. She's not like *Mamère* Yvonne or Grandma Cecily. She's one of those people who need someone else to take care of her, not be responsible for others. Right?"

"Yes," Alain answered. "That's as good a way to say it as any."

"I've been thinking about stuff like that lately. I think maybe when I start looking for a wife, I want to find a girl that will be my partner, too. You know. Not that I couldn't take care of her. And I will. But someone who'll be there for me, too."

"If you find a girl like that, you hang on to her, hear?" Alain said with a smile. "She'll be worth her weight in gold."

"Is that the kind of woman you'd want? I mean, if you marry again?"

Alain hoped the sudden twist of pain he felt in the middle of his chest, right over his heart, didn't show on his face. "Yeah, that's the kind of woman I'd want."

Guy studied him for a long few seconds. "We—Dana and me—we wouldn't mind if you did get married again."

"I'll keep that in mind. Just don't you be in any hurry to find Ms. Right yourself. Okay?"

"Don't worry about that. I was just talking in the abstract, you know. Something that might happen. Someday. Maybe. We've been studying that in school. Right now I just want Dana home. If Mom keeps her word this time, maybe I'll be able to start thinking about being her friend. Someday." Guy pushed away from the table, pocketed his cell phone and walked out of the kitchen.

"I THINK you can count yourself one hell of a father if Dana and Guy grow up and embrace Casey Jo as a friend. It's more than she deserves." Cecily had waited until Guy left the kitchen to come in off the back porch.

"You heard, eh?" Alain asked, not getting up from the table as she poured herself a cup of coffee that looked black enough and strong enough to keep her on her feet another four hours.

"Of course I did. In the first place, I couldn't help but overhear without sticking my head in the dryer. In the second place, I didn't try not to. You're two of the three most important people in my life. I wanted to hear what he had to say about his mother."

"I swear I never knew about her leaving him in the mall like that."

"I'm not surprised it happened, but there's no way you could have known about it." She sat down beside Alain at the table. It had been in the family for almost a hundred years. She'd been raised around this table, so had her mother and aunts and uncles, as well as her own three kids. One of the hardest things she'd had to do after her husband died was to stop setting his place each night.

"He's afraid she'll do something like that with Dana."

"I wouldn't put it past her," Cecily said before she could censor herself.

"Guy asked me why I married her." Alain ran his thumb up and down the side of his water bottle. He was wearing an old plaid shirt of his dad's and he looked so much like him that her throat tightened with tears.

"You thought it was the right thing to do. And I encouraged you." Cecily sighed. "But believe me, I've asked myself that same question a lot of times the past fifteen years. I thought she'd grow up." She looked up from her coffee cup. "I thought you were over Sophie Clarkson and that you and Casey Jo would have as good a chance at making a go of your marriage as anyone else in that situation. I was wrong on both counts, wasn't I?"

He had been staring at a spot on the wall beyond her left shoulder, but now he brought his gaze down to hers.

"I'm still hoping she'll grow up before Dana does," he said, ignoring the other half of her question.

"I'm not holding my breath." She stood up and poured the rest of her coffee into the sink. It was too strong even for her. She couldn't spend half the night lying awake, stewing over those damned stuffed animals again. She had to be on duty at seven the next morning, the Lord's Day or not. She turned around and leaned her hip against the counter. Time to get another worry out of her thoughts and into the open. "Alain, what about you and Sophie?"

"She's heading back to Houston on Monday," he said, pushing back his chair and rising to his feet. He was taller, leaner than his father had been. He took after her side of the family that way, just as Guy did.

"For good?"

He shrugged. "I don't know."

"Did you ask her to stay?" She usually kept her nose out of his love life but she sensed what he felt for Sophie Clarkson was too important to keep quiet about.

"No," he said bluntly. "What can I offer her?" He pushed his hand through his hair, making it stand up on end just as it had when he was a little boy. "My life is pretty much a soap opera right now, Mom, you have to admit that. Even if she was willing to take on a man with two half-grown kids and a perpetual-adolescent ex-wife, there's the problem of her having a life in Houston that she doesn't want to give up."

"Did you ask her that?" Cecily held her breath. Had it gone that far? Had Alain asked Sophie to marry him—again?

"I asked her if she believed in second chances," he said, and the sadness in his voice was so well hidden she suspected no one but his own mother would have detected it.

"Everyone believes in second chances," Cecily whispered.

"That's what I told her." He aimed the empty water bottle at the wastebasket in the corner. "She told me we had our second chance seven years ago when Casey Jo burst into the back of Past Perfect and found us together. She said this was our third time around." He shoved his hands in his pocket. "And three times wasn't a charm. It was three strikes and you're out."

"Oh, Alain, that's not true." She was afraid if she said anything more she'd start to cry, she hurt so badly for him.

"Maybe if things were more settled here I'd be able to convince her of that. But as it is, Dana has to come first." One corner of his mouth ticked up in a travesty of a grin. "It's not like I haven't been here before."

She watched him turn and leave the room and her heart ached for him. The dryer buzzer went off like a hundred angry bumblebees. Automatically she went to take out the load of towels and fold them. It kept her hands busy while her thoughts wheeled around in her brain.

The last thing in the world she wanted to do at the moment was bother him with her own problems. The damned toy animals, in full view of the town now in the window of Past Perfect, would have to wait. Her baby was hurting, and as Alain had just said, your children's welfare came first—even before unfilled prescriptions and jail time.

Maybe she should talk to Sophie, tell her Alain loved her, because she knew with absolute certainty that he did. If she had any inkling that Sophie loved him back, she'd get down on her knees and beg her to stay in Indigo until this mess with Casey Jo was put behind them.

Maybe if she'd done that years ago, things would be different now. But she hadn't wanted to interfere in his love life then any more than she did now. And who knew that Casey Jo was going to show up after six months of silence, looking like she'd swallowed a watermelon and demand that Alain take her back just as though she'd never up and left him and her precious baby boy to follow her own foolish dreams?

Casey Jo had a lot to answer for. Maybe if she explained all that to Sophie it would change her mind?

Or maybe not.

The phone rang and she picked it up, hoping against hope it was her ex-daughter-in-law calling to apologize for not checking in for more than two whole days.

"Cecily, is that you?" It wasn't Casey Jo but her mother.

"It's me, Marie. Have you heard from them?" she asked without preamble.

Her answer was a sigh. "No. I was hoping you had."

"Not a word since Thursday night. Alain is fit to be tied. Casey Jo will have a lot to answer for if she doesn't have Dana back here on the dot of seven tomorrow evening."

"I know," Marie said, and for once she didn't tack on some kind of convoluted excuse for Casey Jo's behavior. "I just hope they're both all right."

"You'd better get yourself down to St. Tim's to say a prayer to back that wish up." Cecily hunched her shoulder to hold the phone against her ear while she continued to fold towels.

"I already have." Her tone changed. "Did you know that Sophie Clarkson put those damned stuffed animals out on display?"

It was Cecily's turn to sigh. "Yes. Guy mentioned it. Dana told her that's what Maude did. She was thinking of the ones that people gave back to her when they took out the meds, I suppose. She used to sell some of them, remember."

"She's got Amelia Prejean to run the shop for her. She's reopening Monday morning." Amelia was about Cecily's age but they were the merest of acquaintances. Hugh's niece had only moved to Indigo the year before, after she retired from teaching school back east somewhere, to help look after her aging uncle. She wasn't going to be any help in getting the animals out of Past Perfect.

"He told me that, too."

"We've run out of time. We'll have to break into the opera house tonight."

Cecily felt tears burn the back of her eyelids, but instead of letting them fall, she punched the pile of folded towels with her fist. It wasn't as satisfying as a good cry, but it didn't make her eyes red, either. "Not tonight. I can't do that. Alain's here. He'll hear me leave and wonder what I'm doing going out at this time of night."

"Tomorrow, then. It's our last chance."

"I won't be home from the hospital until six-thirty or seven."

It was Marie's turn to sound exasperated. "We aren't going to do it in broad daylight."

"But Alain…"

"Tell him you're going to spend the evening with your mother because she's worried about Dana."

"She is worried about Dana," Cecily snapped.

"She's my grandbaby, too, don't forget. She'll be fine. They're just having too much fun to be checking in every five minutes." Cecily ground her teeth but didn't get a chance to respond. "Just do as I say for once," Marie continued. "Tell him you're going to Yvonne's. Your mom will be your alibi."

"How will we get in the place?"

"Leave that up to me."

Cecily felt a chill race up and down her spine. She wasn't in the least bit psychic, but she didn't need to be to know this was going to turn out badly; she'd been convinced of that since the day Maude had died. She just hoped Sophie Clarkson wouldn't end up blaming Alain for what she was going to do.

CHAPTER FIFTEEN

SOPHIE STOOD at the window of her suite at the top of La Petite Maison and looked out at the break in the rain clouds that bathed the grounds in watery sunlight. The silence was so complete that the only competition for the church bells of St. Timothy's calling the faithful to worship from over a mile away were the twitters of a few birds in the oaks beside the house. She cradled a mug of Luc's excellent coffee between her hands and thought a bit wistfully that the next Sunday morning would find her in her kitchen in her condo in Houston, staring at a bare white wall, listening to the muted roar of traffic from the expressway that even her building's soundproofed walls couldn't completely filter out.

She was making the right choice going back to Houston, she told herself. Her grandparents would be home from their trip to Australia on Wednesday and she wanted to be there to greet them. And, of course, she needed to get back to work, as well. Her father had been relieved. She could hear it in his voice when she'd called to tell him she was leaving Indigo as soon as the alarm system was reset and she got Amelia Prejean squared away at Past Perfect.

Perhaps once she was back in her own home, among her own things, the feeling that she was making a terrible mistake leaving Indigo…leaving Alain…would stop niggling at the back of her mind.

Surely, if she were truly, no-turning-back in love with him, she wouldn't be able to just up and walk away? Would she?

Her suitcases were open on the quilt-covered pine bed. She was almost finished packing. She would check out of La Petite Maison after breakfast the next morning, pack her car, make sure Maude's little house was securely locked up and then leave for Houston directly from the store. A knock sounded on her bedroom door.

"One moment, please." She set her coffee mug on the bedside table and opened the door. Luc Carter was standing on the tiny landing outside her room. He was dressed in gray slacks and a black shirt, open at the throat, and looked both elegant and casual at the same time.

"Good morning, Sophie," he said.

"Good morning, Luc. I was just on my way down to breakfast."

"It's ready whenever you are. Actually, I came to tell you that you have a visitor downstairs."

"Alain?" Sophie wished she'd been able to school her tongue to silence when she saw one of Luc's dark, expressive brows rise a fraction of an inch.

"It's a Boudreaux, yes. But not our esteemed Chief of Police. It's his son, Guy."

"Guy? What's he doing out here?"

"He wouldn't tell me," Luc said, stepping back so that she could precede him down the stairs. "Said it was private business between the two of you. I put him at the table in the alcove. You can have a little more privacy there."

"Thanks." She hurried down the steps holding on to the rail. The cypress risers were narrow and steep between the second and third floors of the old house. The enticing smells of crisp bacon and hot coffee greeted her halfway down the main staircase with its beautifully carved mahogany banister. She could hear the clatter of silverware and the sounds of voices from the breakfast room.

She stopped in the archway that separated the small lounge reception area from the breakfast room and scanned the faces that looked up as she came into view. She nodded pleasantly at two of the four couples occupying the second floor rooms of the bed and breakfast as they sat gathered around the big harvest table, and then settled her gaze on Alain's son.

Guy had been watching for her and rose from his chair the moment she appeared. He was wearing jeans, with a bike cuff around his ankle, which explained how he'd gotten out here. He'd ridden his bike from town. He was wearing a white dress shirt and tie and a leather jacket, not the usual Indigo High sweatshirt she was used to seeing him in. Sophie guessed he had just come from mass at St. Timothy's.

She walked over to the table and motioned him back into his seat. "Sit down, Guy. Do you want something to eat?"

He remained standing and shook his head. "No thanks, I already had breakfast. I need to talk to you." His voice was so low Sophie had to bend her head closer to hear him. "I…I have to ask a favor."

"Is something wrong?" She was afraid there must be. Why else would he seek her out here at the B&B on a Sunday morning?

"Yeah. Sort of. Look, could we talk somewhere a little more, you know, private?"

"Of course." She led him into the small, comfortably furnished lounge that doubled as the reception area. She sat down on one of the overstuffed sofas that flanked the stone fireplace and patted the seat beside her. "What's wrong, Guy?"

He looked at her with Alain's deep-blue eyes. "I'm here about Dana and my mom." He reached into his jacket pocket and produced a slim cell phone. He flipped it open, checked the display as though to be sure he hadn't somehow missed a call, then closed the lid and wrapped his long fingers around it.

"You've heard from Dana or your mother? Are they all right? I…I didn't talk to your father at all yesterday." The day before had been one of the longest in Sophie's life. She'd spent it at Maude's house, sorting through her personal possessions, not wanting to leave them behind in an unoccupied house. It had been a bitter-sweet task as memories of her childhood and teen years came back to her with each album page she turned, each memento she packed. She had found herself reaching into her pocket for her own cell phone more than once as she worked, anxious to contact Alain and see if there was any news of Dana, yet at the same time, reluctant to be the one making the connection. She was more than a little afraid she would lose her resolve completely and tell him she would stay with him in Indigo forever.

"My mom called me. Right in the middle of mass." He colored a little, but Sophie pretended not to notice. "Father Joe doesn't like people to have their cell phones on in the church, but I didn't want to take the chance of missing a call. Luckily, I was sitting in the back pew and I got out pretty quick."

"What did Dana have to say? Is she having fun? They aren't still in Orlando, are they?" It was a little after eleven. There was no way Casey Jo could meet Alain's 7:00 p.m. deadline if she was still in Florida.

"No. They're in Biloxi somewhere. I…I have the name and address of the motel."

"That's about two hundred miles or so from here, isn't it? They should make it home in plenty of time."

Guy's face tightened. "Casey Jo's car broke down. Threw an engine rod. They're not going anywhere from the sound of it. And Dana's sick. She's throwing up and crying." He shoved his hand through his dark auburn hair in frustration. "Casey Jo was crying, too. She's not used to taking care of a sick kid. And Dana's a world-class crier. The more she cries, the more she throws up. That's the way she is."

Sophie's heart went out to him. He was a conscientious kid, a born protector and he loved his little sister. He hadn't wanted her to go off with Casey Jo and now his worst fears were being realized. "Where's your father? Has he gone to pick them up?" It was the only reason she could think of that Guy had come to her, to give her word of the situation.

"He doesn't know anything about it. My mom's afraid to call him. Anyway, he's at the other end of the parish. The sheriff called early this morning and said there was a fugitive situation. Three guys broke out of jail in New Orleans. The highway patrol thought they might be heading this way. They've got roadblocks set up all over the south end of the parish. I...I didn't try to get hold of him yet, either."

"Your grandmother?"

"She's working." He set his jaw, another mannerism he shared with Alain. "And Grandma Marie's sleeping. She works 'til 3:00 a.m. on Saturday nights. Besides, her car's a bigger lemon than Casey Jo's." Sophie had an idea now where he was going with this. "I need to borrow a car to go get them and bring them back here before Dad's deadline."

"Your great-grandmother—"

"Would be on the phone to the sheriff or the governor or even the president—whoever it took to get hold of my dad—so fast it would make your head swim. I don't want everyone in town to know what's going on. I need a car to go get them and bring them back to Indigo without anyone finding out. Could you loan me yours?"

"Oh, Guy." Sophie tried to make sense of all the scattered facts he'd laid before her. "I can't do that. In the first place, you don't have a license."

"Grandma Marie would drive it. She's a good driver, really, she is. It's her car that's a junker."

Sophie laid her hand on his for just a second, withdrawing it before she embarrassed him. "I'm sorry, Guy. My firm leases my car. The insurance company won't allow anyone else to drive it. Surely, there are enough policemen to man this roadblock. Call your father. It's an emergency. They'll let him go."

"No." The word exploded out of his throat. "You don't understand. I know Dad would go after them in a heartbeat. But we had this talk. And I understand about my mom better now. I want to give her this chance to show she's doing the right thing. I want to go after her and Dana, not my dad."

Sophie was flattered that Guy had come to her, but she had no idea what Alain would think of her inserting herself into his family's affairs. Perhaps if she had told him she loved him when she had the chance, instead of giving in to her own insecurities, it would be different. As things stood now, she didn't even know if they had a relationship, let alone an ongoing one. "Guy, please let me call your father," she pleaded.

"No. I told you I want to do this myself." He stood up and she had to tilt her head back to meet his eyes. "Look, thanks for listening to me. I'll try to call my friend Skeeter. His older brother's got his own car. Maybe if I buy the gas—"

"No." Sophie made up her mind. She wouldn't think of the personal implications of what she was doing, only of Dana's safety, and Guy's, for that matter. She wasn't going to have Alain's son going on a four-hundred-mile road trip with another inexperienced driver. "I'll drive you. But I insist you inform your father or your grandmother what we're doing, otherwise, no deal. Understood?"

He glanced over his shoulder as one of the couples, a dentist from Dallas and his much younger wife, came into the lounge from the breakfast room. "My mom won't be happy to see you."

"I know. But I think I can handle it."

"I'm not blind. I… You and my dad— Well, I've got eyes, and people around town, they remember—"

"You're right about your father and me. Perhaps one day we'll be more than friends. I honestly don't know right now. But that's all beside the point. It's Dana we should be thinking about. And if you're right about your mother wanting another chance to prove she can be a good mom, she'll 'get along to go along,' as my godmother used to say."

He nodded agreement but didn't look any more convinced than Sophie felt. However, she had no other solution to offer and they both knew it. "I'll try my dad right now." Guy ducked his head and flipped open his phone. "No signal. I'll go outside on the porch and try again. Okay?" His eyes flickered to the other couple, who were asking Luc about the visiting hours for Shadows-on-the-Teche.

"I'll go upstairs and get my purse." She would have to trust him on this, even though she could see his reluctance to inform his father of his plans hadn't diminished.

The dentist and his wife were gone when Sophie came back downstairs, slightly breathless from hurrying. Only Luc Carter remained in the lounge, although she could hear the murmur of voices from the breakfast room.

"Going out with young Boudreaux?" he asked, coming out from behind the antique table that served as a reception desk.

"Yes," Sophie replied, wondering how much she could tell him of her plans. "I'll be gone most of the day." She would finish packing when Dana, and she supposed Casey Jo, were safely back in Indigo.

"Is there any message you care to leave if someone inquires for you?" he asked, the perfect host.

"No message."

"You believe the boy is actually contacting his father then?" He made no attempt to hide the fact he must have overhead at least part of her conversation with Guy.

She looked him straight in the eye. "Yes."

"How far away is she? Boudreaux's ex and the little girl, I mean?" He shrugged. "Half the town knows the woman took off with her to Disney World."

He was probably right about that. "They're somewhere near Biloxi. They've had car trouble and Dana's under the weather, probably from too much excitement and theme-park food."

"And Guy is determined to bring them safely home." A smile lifted the corner of his mouth. "Southern gallantry is alive and well a hundred and fifty years after the fall of the Confederacy." He indicated where Guy, visible through the low windows, was standing on the wide porch, cell phone to his ear. His smile grew broader. "That acorn sure didn't fall far from the tree."

Sophie managed a smile, too. "No," she agreed. "He certainly did not."

IT WAS DARK by the time Alain pulled into his parking space at the municipal building. Main Street was deserted. The General Store was open and the gas station on the corner had its lights on, but the rest of the town had settled in for the evening, staying warm and dry out of the rain and chill wind. He picked up his hat and gathered up his paperwork.

What a hell of a wasted day. Six hours spent manning a roadblock on a backwater road that no one in the parish much used anymore, and that sure wouldn't be on any self-respecting crooks' escape route. But the state boys were running the show, and the sheriff, just following orders, you understand, wasn't above getting a little of his own back as far as Alain was concerned, sending him off to stand guard over skunk cabbage and alligator holes at the back of beyond.

To top it all off, the escaped prisoners had all been recaptured before they ever made it out of the city. The only bright spot in the miserable, wet day was the fact that the sheriff must see him as a potential threat come election time, or he wouldn't have made sure there was no chance in hell that Alain would get credit for apprehending the fugitives if they had got this far north. Small comfort for his aching feet and chilled bones, but it was all he had.

He gathered up his paperwork, dumped it on his

desk to deal with in the morning and headed back out of his cubbyhole office to the front desk, where Damien Homier was just checking in for the night shift. "You two holding down the fort tonight?" he observed, returning his shotgun and ammunition to the gun safe in the corner. He spun the combination lock and initialed the weapons log that Billy Paul held out to him.

"Just the two of us to keep each other awake." Billy Paul, fat, bald and fifty, but still the best drummer in the parish, shoved the weapons log back in the desk.

"I'll be heading out on patrol in another hour or so." Damien Homier was young and eager. He'd make a good cop someday. Now he found Indigo too tame for his liking, but that would change, Alain thought with a wry grin.

"Take care of yourself. I'll be at home if you need me."

"Hey, Chief. Just remembered." Billy Paul grabbed a yellow sticky note that had been affixed to his radio and handed it over the four-foot-high plywood divider that was all that separated them from the citizenry of Indigo. "It's a note from your mom. Says to check your voice mail for messages and to get home right away."

Five minutes later Alain wheeled the Explorer into the driveway. There were lights on all over the house. His mother met him at the kitchen door. "You got my message?" she asked without preamble.

"Yeah, just now. I've had my phone off all day. There wasn't any decent signal out in the boonies where I was, and I didn't want the battery to run down. "What's going on?"

"I don't know." She looked worried but her voice was calm and she moved back into the kitchen in a normal, unhurried manner. Thirty years of working in a hospital ER gave you nerves of steel. "There was a message from Guy on the answering machine when I got home. He's in Biloxi!" Her calm deserted her for a moment as her voice rose. "He was calling from one of those walk-in clinics. It's okay," she said hurriedly. "Dana's sick. Tummy troubles, nothing serious. They're on their way back now, I guess. He's not answering his cell. How in heaven's name did he get to Biloxi? I called Marie but she hadn't heard anything. She's more in the dark than I am."

Alain had tried Guy's cell first thing after he'd turned on his own, but he'd had no better luck connecting than his mother. "I don't have too many more details. Here, listen to Guy's message." She put the cell to her ear. He didn't have to listen. He'd already memorized the words.

Dad, it's Guy. There's a problem. Casey Jo's car broke down. She's in Biloxi and Dana's not feeling well. She wants to get home on time like she promised. I...I told her I'd help. I found someone to take me to get them. It's...it's Miss Sophie. I'll call you back when I get there. Don't worry, Dad. She's a good driver.

The second message was short and to the point: *Dad, my battery's running down. The doctor says Dana's okay. It's about four o'clock. We're heading home.* A slight pause, then the words that had stuck in Alain's brain ever since. *All four of us.*

Cecily handed the phone back to him. "Sophie

Clarkson? He asked her before he called me?" If he hadn't been bone-tired and still getting over the scare of his life from that yellow sticky note, he'd have given a lot of money for a picture of the look of consternation and pique that flashed across his mother's face.

"I'm sure he thought of you first, but even if you could have gotten someone to cover the rest of your shift, it would have taken you at least forty-five minutes to get back here. He was using his head." Alain felt himself beginning to uncoil a little, the cold, hard knot of fear that had settled in his gut thawing slightly. "My guess is that it's got something to do with the talk we had last night. He's trying to make amends for always thinking the worst of her actions all these years."

"That's because she usually does—"

"Mom, that's not going to do any good."

"I know. I know. When do you think they'll be back?" she asked, glancing at the rooster-decorated clock that had hung above the sink for as long as Alain could remember. "It's almost seven."

"It's four hundred miles there and back, or as close as doesn't matter. Probably eight or eight-thirty. Not much sooner than that."

"Four hours cooped up in the same car with Casey Jo," Cecily said, worrying her lower lip. "How will Sophie handle it?" There were other questions he could see lurking in her brown eyes but she didn't ask them.

"I think she'll handle it just fine." But deep inside he wasn't so sure.

CHAPTER SIXTEEN

"MARIE, it's Cecily. I'm calling to ask if you've heard anything from Casey Jo?" She flipped the heavy braid over her shoulder. Maybe it was time to get her hair cut. The weight of it was giving her headaches. Or maybe it was stress. She had surely had enough of that to deal with lately.

"Not a word. But she doesn't have a phone plan. She pays by the minute so she only uses her cell for emergencies. Is everything okay? Are they on their way back home?"

"As far as I know. Alain's here now and he had a couple of voice messages from Guy on his phone. They took Dana to a walk-in clinic. She's doing fine. It was probably just too much of everything. You know she's got a delicate stomach. Evidently, it was Sophie Clarkson who drove Guy to Biloxi."

"Sophie Clarkson?"

"Yes, Sophie." Cecily smiled. She surely must love Alain to have volunteered for such a task, especially if it meant being cooped up in a car with his ex-wife for four or five hours.

"Well, it should be interesting when she butts heads with Casey Jo."

Cecily's smiled faded. "I just wanted to let you know everything's okay," she said rather more sharply than necessary. "Alain thinks they'll be back around eight or so."

"Then, we'd better get moving."

"Moving? What are you talking about?"

"You know perfectly well what I'm talking about. We either get those drugs out of Past Perfect tonight or we forget about it. Sophie Clarkson is reopening the store tomorrow morning. They're fixing the security system. We've been over this and over this."

Stomach acid began to churn and work its way up Cecily's esophagus.

"Go tell Alain you're going over to your mother's to explain what's going on so you don't tie up the phones," Marie instructed. "She'll be your alibi just like we discussed before. Leave your car at her place and walk from there. I'll meet you behind the diner. Bring a flashlight. And, oh yeah, wear black."

She disconnected and Cecily was left with a dial tone ringing in her ear.

Twenty minutes later she was in the alley behind the Blue Moon, waiting for Marie to make an appearance. It was dark and had rained off and on all day so there were puddles here and there waiting to trip her up and soak her shoes. She looked around a little nervously. Even in Indigo, where a lot of people didn't bother to lock their doors at night, it was a scary to be in a dark alley alone.

Cars passed in the street, and she could hear the voices of people coming and going from the General

Store and the gas station, the only businesses open on a Sunday evening, but she still felt alone and vulnerable and it wasn't a comfortable feeling. She had just made up her mind to go home and forget this whole ridiculous business when Marie drove up and parked in her usual space beside the back door of the restaurant. She got out and was momentarily illuminated by the security light above the door.

"Mon Dieu," Cecily breathed. "She looks like Cat Woman." Marie's dark pants and sweater were skin-tight and, damn it, she didn't look half bad for a woman her age.

Cecily stepped out of the shadows. "Why did I have to walk and you drive up and park back here like it was no big thing?" she hissed.

Marie plopped her hand over her heart. "Good Lord, you just scared me out of a year's growth."

"Good, then we're even," Cecily snapped back. "I don't much like standing out here in the dark, either."

"I parked here because it's where I always park and people are used to seeing my car here even when the diner's closed. You left your car at your mother's place so you'll have an alibi." Marie reached into the back seat and pulled out a lumpy bundle tied up in dark cloth.

"What do you have there?" Cecily asked.

Marie shut the car door. "Burglary tools." She started off at a brisk pace. A block up and they would intersect with the alley that ran behind the opera house. As long as no one saw them cross Jackson Street, they would be okay.

"I can't believe we're doing this. It's insane. It's only seven-thirty. No one robs a building at seven-thirty in the evening."

"We are," Marie said.

"We should be doing this in the middle of the night."

"It's as dark as it's going to get. Besides, once Casey Jo and the kids get back, there'll be no getting away again tonight. Not as long as Dana's not feeling well, you know you won't leave her. I told you, this is our last chance. Now stop looking for excuses to wimp out and run home."

"I'm not looking for excuses to wimp out," Cecily insisted, although it was a bald-faced lie.

Marie looked both ways, put her fingers to her lips, and motioned for Cecily to follow her across the deserted street. "Do you really think you could get out of the house in the middle of the night without waking Alain? I bet he sleeps with his eyes open."

"He does no such thing," Cecily insisted loyally. But Marie was right about one thing. Alain was a light sleeper, especially with a fussy child in the next room. He would hear her if she got up and left the house in the middle of the night. "There's quite a bit of traffic around the square," she whispered. "Someone will surely see our flashlights." She was already out of breath and they were still two blocks from the opera house.

"Not unless they're flying by the windows. You know they're at least eight feet off the ground every-where but the lobby."

"I know," Cecily said. Marie had just shot down her

last argument and she couldn't think of anything else to say.

The opera house loomed over them, a dark bulk against the darker sky. The windows caught glints of light from street lamps in the square, but everything else was in shadow.

"How are we going to get inside?" Cecily said under her breath. She hated being so passive but she simply had no idea how to go about breaking and entering.

"There's a window behind the stage with a broken lock."

"How do you know that?" She was completely out of breath now, and her bad knee had begun to ache. Why shouldn't it? Most cat burglars weren't fifty-six-year-old women who had already put in an eight-hour shift in a busy hospital emergency room.

"Your mother told me," Marie hissed back. "Maude told her about it just before she died. She told me at the wake. Maude never had a chance to get it fixed."

"Our lucky day," Cecily said morosely.

"Exactly. That and the fact that Damien Homier's on duty tonight and not Alain. Homier's dumber than a box of rocks."

Cecily didn't share her companion's low estimation of Alain's newest employee's intelligence, but she remained silent. Marie climbed the rickety metal fire escape that crisscrossed the back of the building, pausing at the landing at the top of the first flight of steps. Just as Cecily remembered, there wasn't a window that opened onto the fire escape. The nearest one was at least two feet to the left of the waist-high railing.

"Grab my belt," Marie ordered as she tested the railing. "I need some leverage for this." Cecily grasped her belt with both hands, ignored the pain in her knees, and set her feet. Marie leaned as far over the railing as she could and began to work the thin end of the crowbar under the window frame. Cecily mentally ran through the procedures for treating broken bones and concussion.

With two horrendous squeaks, which Cecily was sure anyone in the town square—and even Damien Homier over at the station—could hear, the window slid open.

"There," Marie said, panting with exertion. "We're in."

"How?" But Cecily was afraid she knew.

"Climb onto the railing and slither through the window on your belly. Ready?"

"I suppose so." Slither? She hadn't been the size to slither through anything for about fifteen years. Now she wished she'd told Marie how to immobilize a broken leg. Or warned the other woman not to let her swallow her tongue when she went into a seizure from landing on her head when she fell out of the window.

Marie climbed onto the railing, angled her body into the window and pushed through. Two agonizing minutes later Cecily landed beside her on the dark, dusty floor. She sat with her back against the wall, gasping for breath and trying to decide if she'd broken a rib or only cracked one.

"Are you okay?" Marie whispered, shining her flashlight straight down at the floor for a brief moment while she searched Cecily's face.

"I think so. You'd better call Alain right now to come and arrest us because I'm not going back through that window."

Marie reached out and hoisted Cecily to her feet. "Put your hand on my shoulder, and don't trip and sprain an ankle. Then we'd really be in trouble. Here's the curtain. Be careful climbing down off the stage."

Cecily kept her mouth shut with an effort. She would like nothing more than to give Marie Lesatz a piece of her mind, but the truth of the matter was she was totally out of her element and Marie wasn't. She was moving through the Stygian blackness as if it was broad daylight. Cecily couldn't see her hand in front of her face.

Light from nearby streetlamps shone in through the high windows of the auditorium, allowing them to see vague shapes in the gloom. They hurried up the aisle toward the dark piles of furniture that Guy and his friends had so painstakingly rearranged to Sophie's satisfaction.

"I'm going to turn on my flashlight," Cecily decided. "This place is a minefield of glass and china. I don't want to break anything."

"Okay," Marie said, not bothering to whisper. "Just keep it pointed down. We don't want anyone glancing up at the windows and seeing our lights flashing around."

Cecily had had enough. "I know that much. What I don't know is how you learned so much about breaking and entering?"

"I watch a lot of TV crime shows."

"That's comforting."

"Turn your light off—I'm going to open the doors. When I do, stay low."

She moved purposefully toward the big double doors, opened one, with more ear-splitting squeals of old hinges, and slipped into the showroom. Cecily wasn't good at crouching so she got down on her hands and knees and crawled behind the counter. Marie was halfway to the big highboy where Sophie had arranged the contraband toys before Cecily began to follow. "They're here," Marie whispered. "Make sure no one's walking by outside. I'm going to have to stand up to get them."

Cecily scurried forward and crouched below the front door. Already three cars had driven by, their headlights giving her palpitations when they flickered through the windows. She lifted her head and looked first right, then left. "Coast's clear," she hissed.

She heard the rustle of plastic as Marie pulled a shopping bag out of her back pocket. She kept her eyes on the street and resisted the temptation of turning her head to watch Marie scoop the toys into her sack.

"Got them!" Marie crowed.

"Wait! A car's coming." Horror tightened Cecily's insides. This time the car passing by wasn't an ordinary one. It was a patrol car. Not Alain's Explorer, thank goodness. But a police car, nonetheless. And it was stopping outside. "It's Damien Homier. He must have decided to start his patrol early. Get down. Hurry!"

She heard a little plop as Marie dropped to the floor. But there was no time for Cecily to get back to the relative safety of the counter and the dark shadows of the auditorium. She scooted behind a table and pulled the lacy tablecloth around her as best she could. Footsteps sounded on the porch boards. A flashlight beam cut across the room. Someone rattled the doorknob. Cecily sucked in her breath and wondered if her heart was beating loud enough to be heard through the door.

Evidently not, because after another rattle, the beefy outline of Indigo's rookie police officer disappeared from the far wall. Cecily couldn't hear his retreating footsteps as he left the porch because the blood was still pounding in her ears. Straining, she heard a door slam and the blessed sound of a car pulling away from the curb.

She caught movement as Marie crawled toward her. She laid her hand on Cecily's arm.

"C'mon," Marie whispered so quietly Cecily could scarcely hear her. "We have to go."

She nodded, not trusting her voice, and crawled as quickly as her aching knees would allow into the musty darkness of the auditorium. Marie eased the crack in the big doors shut and turned the latch so slowly it barely made a protest.

She slumped against the wall, the bag of little animals between her outstretched legs.

Cecily pulled her legs up and laid her forehead on her knees. It had always been so simple: the members of their little smuggling ring got their medication at reasonable prices, Cecily's cousin got five percent of the cost of each prescription from the members of the group for her time and trouble, the toys, relieved of their contraband burden, got a good home with grandkids and nieces and nephews, and everyone went away happy. Well, except maybe for Byron McKee, the town druggist, but you couldn't please everyone all the time.

Marie stood up and held out her hand to help Cecily to her feet. "Come on. We'd better get out of here before Homier decides to check the back side of the building and finds the window open."

"Don't even think it." Cecily shuddered as an image played in her mind's eye of Marie and her, coats over their heads, hands handcuffed behind their backs, being perp-walked into Alain's jail. She didn't watch as much TV as Marie, but she'd seen such arrests often enough on the evening news to make the vision frighteningly real.

Actually, it didn't turn out to be quite that bad.

At least, Cecily thought, as she raised both hands over her head and walked out onto the fire escape ahead of the flabbergasted young policeman, he hadn't caught her with her fanny hanging out of the window, dangling fifteen feet off the ground. No, he'd been waiting halfway up the fire escape, only his shocked face and drawn gun was visible as Marie stuck her head out of the window to reconnoiter their escape route.

"Police," he said, not loudly at all. "Don't move."

"Run!" Marie kicked the bag of stuffed animals blindly in Cecily's direction, then raised both her hands, all the time bent over like a pretzel with her head out the window.

It wasn't a flattering pose, Cecily thought a little hysterically.

"Don't shoot, Damien. It's me, Marie Lesatz."

"Whoever's inside, open the fire escape door slowly and come out with your hands up." Cecily did as she was told, her hands shaking so badly it took two tries to turn the deadbolt on the door.

"Good Lord, Mrs. Boudreaux. Is that you?" The young cop's eyes were as big as saucers in his round face.

"Yes, Damien, it's me," she said. She wished she'd had the courage to take Marie's advice and run into the darkness of the auditorium, but no matter how much they argued and sniped at each other, Marie was her friend and she wasn't going to leave her to face the consequences of their stupidity alone. "Put your gun down, will you? It's scaring me to death."

CHAPTER SEVENTEEN

"THEY'RE BOTH ASLEEP. Thank the Lord. I don't know what I'd do if Dana decided to upchuck on your leather seats."

"They're washable," Sophie replied in a low voice. She had hoped the very mild sedative the urgent-care doctor had given Dana would allow the poor little girl some rest, and it seemed to be working. She wasn't seriously ill, thank heaven, just worn out from too little sleep, too much excitement and too much rich food. She'd kept down the electrolyte drink they'd given her at the clinic, and a little later a protein shake that tasted enough like chocolate milk to pass muster with an exhausted and petulant seven-year-old.

It had been Guy, not her mother, who had talked a pale and teary-eyed Dana into cooperating with the doctor to avoid a time-consuming and scary-to-a-little-girl IV to treat her dehydration. Sophie hadn't been present in the exam room, but the walls of the Biloxi walk-in clinic were paper thin, and both Dana's voice and Guy's carried to where she sat in an uncomfortable plastic chair.

"You'd never get the stink out of them and we both

know it." Casey Jo settled back into the bucket seat of Sophie's Lexus and braced her foot on the dash. "My God, what a day." Sophie kept her attention on the road, watching the approaching headlights of a big semi-rig through the swish-swish of the windshield wipers. The silence lasted for a minute or two and then Casey Jo spoke again. "I suppose I'd better get this over with. There hasn't been time, what with sittin' in the doctor's office and packing the car and all, but I want to thank you for driving Guy all this way to get us."

"It was nothing," Sophie said automatically.

"Bull—" Casey Jo glanced over her shoulder at her sleeping children.

Sophie found their reflections in the rearview mirror at the same time. Dana was curled up against Guy's side. His arm was wrapped protectively around her shoulders while he sprawled in the corner of the seat, his jacket rolled up beneath his head as it rested against the car window. His mouth was open and he was snoring, just a little.

"Bullcrap," Alain's ex-wife replied. "It's a hell of an imposition and I have enough manners to say thank you when someone deserves it. But I don't think you did it just out of the goodness of your heart," she added bluntly.

Sophie had had a lot of time to think about why she had made the trip, and although she tried to tell herself it was only the act of a Good Samaritan, or a good friend, she knew she was lying. She had done it because she loved Alain, and by extension, his children. For that simple, earth-shaking, life-altering reason, and no other.

"You're in love with that stick-up-the-butt ex-husband of mine, aren't you?" Casey Jo wasn't looking at Sophie but staring straight ahead into the gathering night. The other woman hadn't bothered with her hair or makeup today, or more likely just hadn't had the time to spend on herself. Tonight she looked tired, not so young as she once was, and just a little worn around the edges.

Sophie considered not answering her, but didn't give in to the urge to dodge the question. "Yes, I am." If she and Alain did manage to carve out a future for themselves, this woman would be part of it whether Sophie liked the idea or not. She didn't intend to run away from Casey Jo ever again.

"Did he ask you to marry him yet?" Casey Jo shifted a little in her seat, one foot still propped on the dash like a teenager.

"No. We haven't discussed marriage."

"You want him, though, don't you?"

"Yes," Sophie said. "I do want him. With all my heart. I have for a long time somewhere deep inside. But we never did anything to dishonor the vows he made to you, Casey Jo."

She waved her fingers in the air. "Hell, I know that. Alain's too full of himself to sneak around on me."

"Then why did you accuse us of having an affair all those years ago?"

"'Cause I was pregnant and broke and I wanted him back and I knew guilt was the only thing that would hold him to me. Hell, we'd still be married if I hadn't just got fed up with all of it and left town again. Best thing I ever did for myself."

"You gave up your place in your children's lives to chase a dream?"

"And I'd do it again. It's not my fault it's been so long coming. But I still have hope. Vegas is my next stop."

"Why are you coming back to Indigo, then? We were only about twenty miles from where you live, weren't we?"

Casey Jo's expression turned crafty. "That would really put a crimp in your plans if I came back to Indigo for good, wouldn't it? Well, you don't have to worry about that. I have a boyfriend now. He'll be bringing my car to town when it's fixed to pick me up. We're living together. We're going to get married someday," she said just a bit defensively. "We've been together for almost a year. He's a pit boss at the casino where I deal blackjack. He thinks I can make it as a lounge singer. In the big hotels, not fly-by-night joints off the Strip. He's got faith in me. He's helping me look for a new agent. We're heading to Vegas in a couple of months. That's why I wanted to give the kids this treat. After we leave Mississippi, I won't be able to see them again for maybe a long time."

"That's what you really want in life?" Sophie heard herself speak the thought aloud and apologized. "I'm sorry, I shouldn't have said that."

"Don't bother. I might ask you the same thing. You'd give up all this?" Casey Jo indicated the interior of the expensive car, but the gesture was meant to encompass much more: Sophie's job, her condo, her life in Houston.

"To have what you walked away from, you mean?"

Casey Jo blinked as she absorbed the words. "I suppose you think I screwed up with my kids, taking off like I did and leaving them behind."

"I wouldn't have done it," Sophie replied.

"No, I imagine you wouldn't. But then you didn't grow up on the wrong side of the tracks in a one-horse town with your mom tending bar nights and your dad so long gone you can't even remember what he looked like. Besides, they'll thank me for it someday when I'm rich and famous. When they're grown up we'll all be friends."

Sophie thought of the hard set to Guy's face when they'd finally tracked his mother and sister down at the shabby motel on the outskirts of Biloxi. The place bore signs of past hurricane damage in its mismatched shingles and two-toned aluminum siding. She could still hear the angry note in his voice as he argued with her to take Dana to the doctor to get her help for the retching that convulsed her little body. It would take a bigger miracle than Casey Jo's winning a Grammy for that wish to come true. "I pray you're right about that."

"Lordy, you're a real goody-goody, aren't you," Casey Jo said with a flip of her dark hair. "You deserve to be saddled with Alain. You're two of a kind." She peered over the console at her sleeping children. Sophie pretended not to see the mixture of pleasure and pain on her face. Her voice was quieter when she spoke next, less brash and confrontational. "I'm not a complete fool. They're better off with their father and we both know it."

As she continued to watch, Dana stretched and yawned, then sat up rubbing her eyes. "Mommy, where are we?"

"About halfway home, Snickerdoodle. Are you going to be sick again?"

Dana closed her eyes and scrunched up her little face. Sophie scanned the roadside for a place to pull off, just in case. "No," she said after a few moments. "I'm not going to be sick. But I'm thirsty. And I have to go to the bathroom."

"We'll get off at the next exit," Sophie promised as Guy stretched and came awake, too.

"Where are we?" he asked, peering into the late-winter darkness that had fallen while she and Casey Jo talked.

"About an hour from Indigo. We should be home by eight-thirty or a little before."

"Just an hour and a half late." He sounded pleased with himself, as though he'd accomplished what he'd set out to do.

"I'm hungry," Dana said with a little quaver in her voice. "My tummy's growling."

"There's a McDonald's at this exit," Sophie said doubtfully.

"I could do with a couple of quarter pounders and a biggie fries," Guy prompted.

"The doctor said Dana should only have soft, light foods for a day or two. I don't think a burger or chicken nuggets qualify, do you?" Sophie deferred to Casey Jo as the children's mother, however reluctant she was to assume the responsibilities that went with it.

"She'd heave them back up in five minutes," Casey Jo agreed in her blunt way.

"Maybe a little ice cream and one of the protein shakes they gave us at the clinic will hold her until we get back to Indigo."

"Or yogurt," Dana piped up. "They have yogurt with fruit on top. I like it."

"Definitely on the mend." Casey Jo's smile was genuine and Sophie returned it. She doubted they would ever be friends, but maybe they could get along for the children's sake, if not Alain's.

There I go again, planning for a future that might not come to pass.

"I think I'll top off the gas tank when we stop."

"It's over half full—more than enough to get to Indigo," Casey Jo observed.

"I'm leaving for Houston tomorrow. It will save me doing it then."

Casey Jo glanced into the backseat. Guy was busy helping Dana into her sweater and shaking the wrinkles out of his jacket. They weren't paying attention to the adults in the front seat, at least for the moment. "I figured you'd be staying in Indigo."

"I can't," she said as bluntly as Casey Jo would have. "Not yet, at least."

ALAIN WOKE from a slight doze. He'd been sitting in the wing chair that occupied the place of honor in front of the big window in the living room. No one ever sat in it except at Christmas and Thanksgiving, when the house was overflowing with his sisters and their families, aunts, uncles, assorted cousins and sometimes a neighbor or two, but it commanded a view of the street in both directions and made the perfect observation point.

He hadn't planned to fall asleep, but it had been a long day and his body had overruled his mind. The house was dark and quiet, no television, no radio, no one talking on the phone. He realized his mother hadn't come back from *Mamère* Yvonne's. She'd been gone for over an hour and he was surprised they both hadn't returned to keep vigil with him. He glanced at the luminous dial of his watch. A few minutes after eight o'clock. He hadn't heard anything from Guy or Sophie since they'd left Baton Rouge. If Sophie drove the speed limit, and Dana hadn't started vomiting again, they should be pulling into the driveway any time.

With Casey Jo in tow.

He stood up, laced his fingers together palms out, and stretched, then shoved his hands in the pockets of his jeans. He walked to the front door and flipped on the porch light. He couldn't help wondering how Sophie was handling the drive back with his ex-wife riding shotgun.

Headlights speared down the street. He felt his heart kick up a beat or two as a car slowed and turned into the driveway. It wasn't his mother's Blazer but a low-slung Lexus. Sophie's car. He was out the door before it came to a stop. The back passenger door opened and Guy got out, unwinding to stretch his arms high over his head as Alain had just done. A moment later he ducked back inside to re-emerge with Dana clinging to his neck, her legs wrapped around his waist.

"Daddy," she called, then must have remembered she

didn't feel well and laid her head on her brother's shoulder. "Daddy, I'm sick," she said in a much less robust tone as Alain descended the porch steps to meet them.

He held out his arms and she tumbled into his embrace. "I throwed up and throwed up."

"I can tell," he said, wrinkling his nose. "I think you got some in your hair."

She nodded solemnly. "I did, and all over my clothes. We had to wrap them up in a plastic bag. They smell awful." She dropped her head on his shoulder and started to sob. "I missed you. I don't like to be sick when you're not there."

Alain looked over the top of her head to see Casey Jo coming around the front of Sophie's car in time to hear Dana's last words. Sophie was standing with her hand on the open driver's door. She had heard, too. She glanced at Casey Jo's back and pity filled her eyes.

Sophie would never neglect a child of hers the way Casey Jo did Dana and Guy, not as long as she had breath in her body. Alain was as sure of that as he was that the sun would rise in the east come morning.

"We got back pretty darn close to your deadline," Casey Jo said, ignoring Dana's remarks, although there was no way she could have missed hearing them.

"Only because Sophie was willing to make the trip with Guy."

"I was going to say I appreciate what she did for us if you would have given me time to take a breath of air before you jumped down my throat." Her eyes glittered with anger, and beneath that a shadow of hurt and regret. Maybe she did realize what she was missing out on with Guy and Dana, but she would never admit it.

Guy was busy taking suitcases out of the trunk, but Dana had lifted her head from Alain's shoulder to listen to what was being said by the adults. "We'd better take you inside and get you cleaned up and settled for the night. Have you had anything to eat?"

"We stopped at McDonald's. I had ice cream and yogurt. I'm tired. I want to go to sleep. Where's Grandma?" she asked as Alain turned to remount the porch steps with her still in his arms.

"Sophie, will you wait?" He was afraid she'd drive off if he didn't ask her not to.

Casey Jo swiveled her head to stare at Sophie, then turned back to him and held out her arms. She rolled her eyes. "You're pathetic. Here, give her to me. I can still find my way around this house. I'll put her to bed then call my mom to come and get me. You can have a few minutes to take one last stab at talking Sophie here into staying in this godforsaken burg." Casey Jo snorted as Dana unwound her arms from around his neck and settled into her outstretched ones. "Good luck."

"Don't be long, Daddy. I want you to tuck me in." Once more he thought he saw a shadow of hurt flit across Casey Jo's face, but if he did, it lasted only a moment.

"After all the money I spent on you at Disney World, you still want your daddy to tuck you in?" she said in a teasing voice.

Dana wasn't buying it. "Yes," she said, and slithered out of Casey Jo's arms to march up the steps on her own.

"Ungrateful brat," Casey Jo said, but her laugh was brittle.

"I'll be right up." Alain stayed where he was, his eyes holding Sophie's.

"Go to her, Alain. We can talk later." It was hard to read her expression or the neutral tone of her voice.

"I'll help Casey Jo get her ready for bed," Guy said, coming up beside them with suitcases in both hands. "Where's Grandma? I figured her and Grandma Marie would both be here waiting by the curb."

"I don't know where Marie is. Grandma Cecily is at *Mamère* Yvonne's. I expected them both back here a good forty minutes ago."

"I'll give them a call when I get inside." Guy looked from Alain to Sophie and back again.

"Thanks for all your help today, Miss Sophie."

"You're most welcome, Guy." Her voice warmed. "And I think it's time you called me Sophie. I don't know about you, but after today I would like to think we've become good enough friends to dispense with the formalities."

Guy glanced at Alain, gauging his reaction. Alain gave his son a slight nod.

"Thanks, Sophie. And I really do appreciate what you did for me. I…I have some money from my job helping at the B&B." He blushed slightly. "And Past Perfect. I'd like to pay for the gas we used today."

Alain could see Sophie debating how to answer. If she brushed aside his son's offer with a polite refusal, it would make him feel beholden to her. If she agreed to the payment, it would probably wipe out Guy's small savings account. But he had asked a very big favor of her and Alain wanted him to be aware of what a trip like that cost in time and money.

"Thank you for offering, Guy," she said, giving the boy one of her wonderful smiles. "Perhaps we can work something out. I'm going back to Houston, you know, and Ms. Prejean will be running Past Perfect. I'd like to think she could call on you for any help she might need. That would mean so much more to me than money."

Alain clamped his back teeth together to keep from smiling at the ill-concealed look of profound relief on Guy's face as he digested her suggestion. "I'd be glad to help out at the shop. I'll stop by tomorrow after school and introduce myself and leave Ms. Prejean my cell-phone number."

"That will be a real load off my mind."

"I'd better go help Casey Jo with Dana or she'll have her so worked up she'll start puking again." He caught Alain's eye as he walked by lugging Casey Jo's big suitcase and Dana's little one. "She's taking off for Vegas again, did you know that?"

"No," Alain said. "That's news to me."

"Yeah, it was to me, too. Like it worked out so good the last time, right? She's got a boyfriend and she says he's going to get her a job singing there." He rolled his eyes. "Oh yeah, what we talked about the other night? She didn't pass the test."

Alain watched him climb the steps to the house, then turned and walked toward Sophie. She was still standing behind her car door, almost as if she was using it as a shield.

"Did you catch the bad guys?" she asked, curling her hands over the door frame and resting her chin atop them.

"They never got out of New Orleans," he said, not even trying to hide his disgust at the wasted effort. "I'm for sure running for sheriff the next election after today's fiasco."

"You'll probably win," she said, and smiled.

"I'd like to add my thanks to Guy's for what you did today."

"You're welcome. I hoped you wouldn't think I was taking too much on myself doing it."

"Why *did* you do it?" He moved in a little closer, maneuvering around the car door so that she had to turn to face him. "Do you have a Good Samaritan complex?"

"I wanted to help Guy, yes…" She looked down at his chin. "But that wasn't the only reason." After a moment she lifted her gaze to his again, and his heart almost stopped beating in his chest. Her gray-blue eyes were luminous with an emotion he was afraid to put a name to. He reached out to take her in his arms, the neighbors be damned.

His cell phone rang. Alain wanted to ignore it, to throw it down on the ground and stomp on it, but he reached for it instead. Only his mother, Guy and the dispatcher at the station had the number. Duty demanded he take the call.

"Boudreaux here," he growled, his eyes locked with Sophie's, unwilling to let her look away.

"Chief, it's Homier," came the uncertain voice of his

rookie patrolman. "I need you down here at the station, ASAP."

"What's up?" Unless it involved murder or mayhem Alain had no intention of leaving the spot where he was standing until Sophie Clarkson agreed to be his wife.

"I don't know quite how to tell you this."

"Try just spitting it out."

"Chief, I've got your mother and mother-in-law down here in the lock-up. I caught them red-handed breaking into the opera house."

CHAPTER EIGHTEEN

ALAIN COULDN'T BELIEVE his eyes as he stepped through the frosted-glass door that led from the main office space of Indigo's police station to the small holding area. The surroundings themselves were familiar enough, consisting of a single room with green cinderblock walls and a darker green linoleum-tile floor. There were two cells and an open area furnished with a wooden desk and chair. Damien Homier sat behind the desk keeping watch over the two women in the farthest cell.

His mother and ex-mother-in-law locked up in his own jail. It was a sight Alain had never expected to see.

"Details, Homier," Alain barked, fixing his gaze on his subordinate's red face. "And unlock that cell. They're not going anywhere."

"That's what we told him," Cecily said, rising from the cot where she'd been sitting, her face flaming with embarrassment as she caught sight of Sophie following Alain into the holding area.

"He handcuffed us," Marie huffed as the rookie surged to his feet and hurried to do his superior's bidding.

"There were two of you," the young man explained hastily. "I couldn't take the chance on you escaping."

"It's standard procedure," Alain said, cutting Marie off before she could launch into a tirade on his officer's failings. "What the hell were you two doing breaking into the opera house?"

Cecily glanced at Marie, then her eyes strayed to the ordinary plastic grocery bag resting on the scratched and stained wooden table. "We were just retrieving some things that were left there by mistake."

Alain went over and looked into the sack. He could feel Sophie peering over his shoulder. The sack was filled with the small overpriced stuffed animals from Past Perfect. "What the hell is it with these things?" Alain asked, picking up the lopsided frog, a price tag of eighty-two dollars tied to its leg, that he'd examined briefly a few days before.

"There's over two thousand dollars' worth of animals in that bag according to their tags," Homier said a shade defensively. "I didn't find anything else on their persons."

"You patted down my mother?" Alain couldn't quite get his mind around that image.

"Not a full pat-down," the patrolman hurried to explain. "Just their coat pockets. In case, you know, they were carrying concealed."

Homier was a good kid, an Iraq veteran, an MP just as Alain had been. But he bet the poor guy had never been involved in a collar like this one before. He waved off the stammered explanation his patrolman was attempting and transferred his attention to his mother.

"Mom. Marie. I want the whole story, every detail. Now." He emphasized the words with a little shake of the frog in their direction.

"They're our property," Marie said, tears filling her eyes. "We were only trying to get back what was ours."

"But if they were yours, why didn't you just ask me for them?" Sophie's eyes widened as she glanced over at him. "I'm sorry. I should let you ask the questions."

"Go ahead. It's your place that was broken into." He realized at that moment he was wearing his "cop face," as Casey Jo had always termed it. She hated it. He imagined the other women in his life did, too, but it came with the territory. He bet Sophie would get used to it, though. She was that kind of woman. But this time he was interrogating his own mother, so he made a conscious effort to relax. First, though, he gave his subordinate one more long, hard look. "I think we can all agree this will be off the record."

The young cop held up a hand as though he were taking an oath. "Sure thing, Chief." He folded his hands at his middle, hooking his thumbs in his belt and stared off into space as though he had just become invisible.

"Mrs. Boudreaux," Sophie began.

"Cecily, please."

"Cecily." Sophie returned the older woman's smile. "Please explain to us what's going on with these animals. They're cute, but the workmanship doesn't match the price tags. And, well, they simply aren't the kind of merchandise my godmother carried at Past Perfect. If they belong to you, why didn't you just ask for them the first time you came into the shop?" She picked the furry kitten out of the sack, turned it over in her hand and scanned the tag. "Sixty-seven dollars. I just don't understand."

"Squeeze it," Cecily said. "Squeeze its stomach."

Sophie did as Alain's mother directed. "What's in here?"

"It's a pill bottle," Marie said. "We're smuggling drugs in them."

Alain felt his mouth drop open and shut it so hard his teeth knocked together. Homier coughed as though something had caught in his throat.

"You what?" Alain thundered. "You mean this frog is a mule?" He looked down at the toy he was still holding. He gave the frog a squeeze and felt something hard and cylindrical beneath his fingers.

"What?" Cecily looked confused.

"A mule is someone or something drug dealers use to smuggle drugs," Marie hissed, rolling her eyes. "Don't you ever watch the news?"

Alain pulled a penknife from his pocket and slit the frog open. A brown pill bottle popped out of the stuffing. He read the label, blinked and then read it again. "Yvonne Valois! Bisophl—?" How in the hell did you pronounce a word like that? It must have at least half a dozen syllables.

"It's your grandmother's blood pressure medicine, Alain," Cecily stated defiantly. "We're not smuggling *illegal* drugs. We're smuggling *medicine*. From Canada."

"Why in hell?"

"Because it's too expensive to buy them here," she

said. "Or the government won't okay its use, like what was in the teddy bear. I...I took it that day Dana and I came into the shop, Sophie. It was cancer medicine for W—"

"Don't rat him out, Cecily," Marie warned.

"Okay." Cecily looked as if she wanted to cry but pride wouldn't allow herself to. "Most of the people who have drugs in those toys don't have health insurance, or plans with drug coverage, or they're too young for Medicare to help. We all used to order our drugs separately, but a couple of years ago the feds started sending nasty letters warning us it was against the law."

"And why that is, I'll never know," Marie broke in. "I thought buying stuff at the best possible price was the American way." She folded her arms under her breasts and glared at Alain. "It's none of the government's business where I buy my cholesterol medicine. Or at least it shouldn't be," she added a bit less passionately.

"Oh, Alain. Sophie. I'm so sorry. We never thought this would happen. If Maude had lived one more day..." Cecily spread her hands in an apologetic gesture to Sophie, who nodded her understanding. "The animals would have been out of the store and into the hands of the people who have already paid for the medications inside them."

"I still don't see where we did anything wrong, just collecting what's our own," Marie said mulishly.

"You illegally entered private property and removed articles from that property without the permission of the owner." Some of the tightness had left Alain's shoulders and back, though he didn't allow himself to smile. "Property valued at a substantial sum. Without verifiable proof of ownership, we're looking at a felony charge, I'm afraid."

"There's an inventory list somewhere. My cousin always sent them separately. But you know how Maude—" Cecily bit her lip. "Felony?" She sounded as though her brain had only just registered the word. "Do you really mean to send us to jail?"

"We actually did Sophie a favor," Marie insisted. "What if someone else had found that broken window latch? That fancy alarm system is only wired up to the ground-floor windows. Real crooks could have broken in and stolen everything. Set the place on fire. And wouldn't that have caused a hell of an uproar?"

"What if I refuse to press charges," Sophie said. "Then what happens?"

"I suppose we could lower the charges to criminal trespass."

"Alain!"

"Homier, have you filed your report on this incident?" Alain turned his head to regard the younger man.

"Umm…" Damien's face grew red once more. "Well, as a matter of fact, sir, I have not. I…I wasn't quite certain how to…um, proceed," he finished in a rush.

"Was there property damage?"

"Like they said, the latch was broken on the window, but it would be hard to prove they did it. There wasn't any damage to the window frame from the outside. That I can say for sure."

"I should check for wants and warrants," Alain said.

"I've never even gotten a speeding ticket and you know it," Cecily said, sensing the crisis had passed.

"Me, neither," Marie seconded. "Well…maybe a few speeding tickets."

"Since it's a first offense for both of you, and neither of you have prior criminal records, if Sophie agrees I think we can consider the case closed."

"I'm certainly willing," Sophie said quickly. "Nothing was damaged, and you did me a favor finding the broken window latch. Let's all go home." She handed Cecily the bag of stuffed animals. "I believe these are yours."

"Thank you." Cecily's eyes filled with relief.

"From me, too," Marie said, peering into the bag as though to make sure all the animals were there. She took the bag from Cecily and held it out to Alain. "The frog, please. Your grandmother is waiting for her blood pressure medicine."

It was Alain's turn to feel the color creep up his neck. He dropped the gutted frog and the medicine bottle in the sack as though they were suddenly red-hot.

"I'll drive you home, Mom."

"My car's at your grandmother's. She…was supposed to be my alibi."

Once more Officer Homier made a choking sound in the back of his throat and looked as if he wished he were anywhere else on earth but where he was.

"Mother, that's enough—don't say another word," Alain cautioned in an exasperated tone. "You have the right to remain silent, remember. I'll drive you over to

Mamère's to pick up your car. Marie, do you want to come with us? Casey Jo is at my house with Dana."

"Thanks, Alain. I'll walk. My car's just behind the diner. I'll meet you at the house, if that's okay. I do want to see our little Snickerdoodle and make sure she's all right."

"I'll ride with Marie," his mother said hurriedly. "It'll save you a trip. Are we free to go?"

"Promise me this will be your last shipment of smuggled drugs," he said. "If the others want to keep ordering their medications from Canada, I can't stop them. But I can't have a smuggling ring working under my nose. Understand?"

"But…"

"Look, I don't make the laws. You guys have a good network set up here. Put it to use. Start lobbying Baton Rouge and Washington to change the law. That way everyone will benefit and I won't have to bail my mother out of jail anymore."

SOPHIE MEANT to go straight to the B&B when she left the police department, but instead she found herself pulling up in front of Past Perfect. The moon was out, the clouds having been swept away by a cool breeze while she and Alain were dealing with his mother and Marie.

She leaned her hands on the steering wheel and smiled. What an extraordinary day it had been. She hadn't been so tired in a long time. But it was a good tired, the kind that came from accomplishing things. She was good at accomplishing things. She could juggle a dozen balls in the air at a time if she had to. She could make this work. In a few minutes she would drive out to the River Road and La Petite Maison, finish packing and then soak in a hot tub, but first she wanted to talk to Alain. She had no doubt he would be along in a minute or two, and this seemed the place to do it.

She looked up at the opera house as she got out of the car. The weather vane on top of the cupola glinted with hints of copper in the moonlight. The building needed work, a lot of it, but it still had life within its walls. She pulled the keys out of her pocket and unlocked the doors. She stepped inside to the now-familiar smell of potpourri and times past. The streetlight outside gave her enough light to see her way through the crowded displays, but she would have to make sure Amelia Prejean left a lamp or two on when she closed up in the evenings.

She was certain now that she wouldn't close Past Perfect. But she had begun to wonder if it should continue in this location. Maude had opened her business here when the opera house was in danger of being neglected to the point of ruin. Her lease money had kept it going. But now it was time to change, time to stop talking and planning and start to act. Perhaps the absentee Canadian landlord would be more inclined to sell the building to the development committee if it didn't have a tenant? After all, it seemed that he had little interest in the opera house as long as Maude's lease money paid for the very minimal upkeep he was willing to perform. She glanced out at the darkened stores that lined the main square. Surely one of those vacant businesses could house Past

Perfect and give her the space to spread out her inventory, showcase it so people could fully appreciate it.

She would ask Alain what he thought.

She continued into the auditorium, leaving one of the big carved doors open to the soft light of a Gone-with-the-Wind lamp that she switched on as she passed. Here, too, moonlight softened the darkness just enough to make out the rows of seats and the midnight folds of the stage curtains framing the black rectangle of the stage. Around her she sensed the inventory Guy and his friends had so carefully arranged for her. She would still send the fainting couch and one or two other items to the New Orleans dealer the appraiser had recommended, seed money for new merchandise and for Maude's pickers to head back out onto the estate-sale circuit, but the rest would stay here.

Including the Delacroix fiddle that she hoped Alain would play for her.

She heard him then, walking up the steps of the opera house, opening the door. She turned, wondering if he could see her in the deeper shadows of the auditorium, watching as he came unerringly toward her, a darker, more substantial outline in the myriad of shadows surrounding her.

"Sophie?" His voice was low and rough. Goosebumps rose on her arms and she rubbed the skin to soothe the tingle. They had waited so long to be together. Circumstances dictated they wait longer still, but only a short while.

"I'm in here, Alain." She stepped into a small pool of moonlight slanting down from one of the high windows.

He moved toward her. "I saw your car parked out front. I was hoping you wouldn't go back to the B&B right away."

"I've been waiting for you. Is Dana all settled in?"

"She's in the bathtub now with Mom and Marie hovering over her. She's ordered up a snack of toast and warm milk, which she promises she won't throw up. My grandmother is making Casey Jo uncomfortable in the kitchen and Guy, his quest completed, has shut himself into his bedroom with his CD and earphones."

"He handled himself really well, Alain. I want you to know that."

"And Casey Jo didn't."

"She did the best she could."

"It won't be good enough for the kids."

"I know, and I'm sorry, but it's not your fault."

"I'll try to remember that. I promised to be back in time to tuck Dana in." A note of regret tinged his words.

"Of course you need to be there to tuck her in. I don't think it will take us all that long to settle what's between us." She smiled but he couldn't see that. He stayed where he was, just inside the doors.

"You're still planning to return to Houston tomorrow?"

"I have to go back."

She saw, or sensed his brows snap together in a frown. "If you're leaving, what more do we have to say to each other, Sophie?"

"Many things." Quietly, surely, Sophie moved toward him. For the last few days she had been the one who was undecided, who couldn't see clearly what she wanted in life. No more. Today she had seen all that she wanted, all that she could have if she only had the courage to open her mouth and speak three small words.

"But I'll start with just one thing. I love you, Alain. Ever since that first summer. Even when I didn't want to. Even when I shouldn't have, part of me has been in love with you."

"Then why are you leaving?" He was still frowning. She reached up and smoothed her fingertip over the furrows that were etched between his eyes.

"Because I have a life in Houston that I need to deal with. My parents. My job. How I'll manage them in the future. I thought a lot about it on the trip out to Biloxi. I don't want to quit what I'm doing, Alain. Big universities have whole departments to do what I do, but not every institution can afford that kind of expenditure. That's where I come in. I wine and dine and sweet talk. And point out just what a great contribution the prospective donors would be making to the future. I keep it up until I get the endowment for the library or the science lab. Or even the new stadium." She smiled. "I'm good at it. I do good. But there's got to be a way to keep doing it from here. With you. I...I just need some time to figure out how."

"I know you can do it, Sophie. God, I thought you were going to tell me you couldn't handle everything me and my kids threw at you these past couple of days. I thought you might cut and run like Casey Jo. I'll never underestimate you like that again."

"See that you don't."

His strong arms closed around her. "It's going to be a hell of a ride, Sophie. Are you ready for it?"

"More than ready. It's what I want most in the world. Here. Now. Always." His mouth came down on hers and she knew that she was destined to stay in Indigo all her life.

"We'll need a place to live," he said when the kiss ended, and she was pleased to hear the huskiness in his voice matched the breathlessness of her own. "Would you be willing to sell Maude's house to the right buyer?"

"It's too small for a family, Alain," she said regretfully. They hadn't spoken of that either, but she knew there would be babies for them, brothers and sisters for Dana and Guy.

"It's not too small for my mother," he said, threading his hands through her hair. "I've got the feeling she's ready to get out of the big old house and I'm ready to fill it with more babies. How does that sound to you?"

"Exactly what I was thinking."

"Good, then that's settled. Anything else we've forgotten?"

"A wedding would be nice," she said as he began to nuzzle her neck.

"We'll manage that, too. Just not a big country-club one, okay?"

"Okay. And you could say you love me, too."

His arms tightened almost painfully. His lips found hers in another breath-stealing kiss. "I've been saying it, or trying to, for the past three weeks. I love you, Sophie. I always have. I always will."

"Then everything's settled," she said, resting her forehead against his shoulder.

"Well, maybe one more thing." He tilted her head back, his breath soft against her mouth. "Would you wear that corset for me now and then?"

Sophie smiled, her answer swallowed up by his next kiss. Softly, very quietly, perhaps only in her head, she heard a woman's voice begin to sing, sweet and low. Sophie had never thought the opera house haunted, but maybe it was and if not by the spirits of the two lovers who had built it, then by the music that had been made here in the past. Music that would fill this place in the future—if she had anything to do with it.

HOTAL MARCHAND
Four sisters.
A family legacy.
And someone is out to destroy it.

A new Harlequin continuity series continues
in March 2007 with
A SECRET LIFE
by Barbara Dunlop.

As far as Joan Bateman is concerned, life as she'd known it is over. For years she's lived with a dual identify. The people in Indigo know her simply as their neighbor, but to crime mystery readers, she's the best-selling author, Jules Burrell. But once her secret is leaked, the media, her fans and Anthony Verdun, her New York agent, all descend on the sleepy little town. Anthony is bent on using the publicity to promote Joan's latest book, but it's when the plot turns out to be more fact than fiction—and the murderer sets his sights on Joan—that the relationship between author and agent becomes much more personal. This is one crime that mystery writer Joan Bateman can't solve herself....

Here's a preview!

WHATEVER IT WAS, she'd retain her composure. She'd draw on years of poise and practice learned at her mother's knee and keep her feelings bottled tight inside.

"There was a leak," Anthony said.

She mentally shifted gears and glanced up at the ceiling. "Here?"

His shoulders dropped, and he shook his head. "Not that kind of leak."

"Oh."

"An information leak."

His point wasn't quite computing. "Information?"

He stepped closer. "Information about you." He paused. "Personally."

And then she got it.

It was like being struck with a lightning bolt. "*No*," she rasped, shaking her head in denial as the breath hissed out of her body.

Heather's words screamed through her brain. *What were you thinking?*

At this moment, Joan didn't honestly know what she'd been thinking. She'd put her faith in Anthony. She'd trusted him when he said he'd take care of her.

Now, she stared up at him, feeling as though she was seeing him for the very first time, wondering how he could have turned on her. "How could you—"

"Not *me*." A look of horror came over his face.

"Who else?" It couldn't have been anyone else.

He didn't answer.

"Who else knew?"

"There was a confidential file."

"You wrote it down?"

Blind trusts and numbered companies from here to Switzerland, and he wrote it down?

His eyes turned bleak, and he raked a hand through his hair. "Joan, I am so…"

She wanted to rant. She wanted to rave.

But she knew that wouldn't change a thing. All she could control now was how she reacted.

She called on every ounce of composure she could muster and compressed her lips. She had to think. There had to be something they could do, some way to salvage the situation.

"Who else knows?" she asked hoarsely. There was her sister, obviously. There was Anthony. There was the person with the confidential file and two lawyers in Atlanta.

Anthony glanced down at his feet and shifted.

"Who knows?" she repeated. She'd figure out exactly what they were dealing with and they'd take steps to control the problem.

He glanced back up. And then he sighed. "The greater readership of the *New York Times*."

She staggered back. "It's…"

"In the paper. Yesterday."

Oh no. No, no.

"And CNN picked it up this morning."

It was her own fault. She'd grown complacent. After ten years, she thought she was home free. She thought the secret would stay locked behind the corporate screen Anthony had built forever.

So with *Bayou Betrayal,* she'd let loose. She cringed. "It has a *bondage* scene."

"Yeah, but that's the antagonist."

"My mother's going to read it. My *grandmother's* going to read it."

"Joan." His voice sounded far away. "I know we can make this work."

After a second, his words registered.

Make it work?

"You sure it wasn't you?" she asked.

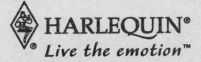

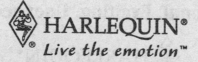

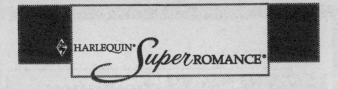
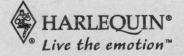

Harlequin Historicals®
Historical Romantic Adventure!

*From rugged lawmen and
valiant knights to defiant heiresses
and spirited frontierswomen,
Harlequin Historicals will
capture your imagination with
their dramatic scope, passion
and adventure.*

*Harlequin Historicals...
they're too good to miss!*